CHURCHILL
PUBLISHING LIBRARY

"Therefore, do not worry about tomorrow, for tomorrow will worry about itself. Each day has enough trouble of its own."
Matthew 6:34

PROLOGUE

Warehouse buildings create a mountain range of concrete and glass down the industrial district street. Window after window of cold glass reflects the dark night sky. Only one building emits a warm glow from within the massive structure. Inside, the floor is illuminated by rows of suspended lighting.

Bullet lies exposed, battered, bruised, unconscious, with blood dripping from his wounds. To the city he was a hero, yet Bullet's image of strength has been destroyed by the same evil he has sworn to keep the city safe from. His mind begins to tremble in fear of death and what will lie ahead for his city once their protector is gone. He strains to wake up from his dream state, only to realize the true nightmare that is his reality.

A well-dressed man—and known killer—stands guard over Bullet. Joe is his name. The darkness of his eyes and his sagging cheeks combine with a blistered frown that oozes bitterness.

"You want Babu to take him out?" Joe asks The Boss.

Babu is just to the side of Joe, a massive figure towering over the small man. Babu leans down to speak at his boss's level. His baggy overalls wrinkle into a mass of fabric, and the collar of his undershirt crawls up his fat neck. His haggard mug twists as he asks: "Uh, where you want me to take him?"

"He means kill him, you big goof!" The Boss corrects her half-witted hit man. She draws from her cigarette in its slender holder. The smoke plumes from beneath her black, brimmed hat. She takes a step toward Bullet, her tight, floor-length white dress stretching with the movement. Her second step lands on her cigarette as it hits the ground from her casual flick.

Babu watches the last line of smoke fade away before his eyes slither up The Boss's long, beautiful legs. Starting at the heel of her shoe, he follows every curve of her black stockings. When his eyes reach the top of the slit in her dress, Babu shakes his head clear.

Joe reaches for his pistol, tucked inside his coat pocket. With the overhead lights reflecting off the chrome of the gun, he smiles devilishly. He stares down at their broken enemy, ready to finish what they started.

But The Boss slows Joe's attack. She pulls a perfect white daisy from behind her ear, letting it slide across her flawless pink cheek. "Now, now, boys, let's be fair," she says. Removing one petal at a time, she recites: "We kill him, we kill him not . . ."

She stops reciting and stares out into the room. She hears the noise of the warehouse—a printing press. Once faded in the distance, now pounding in her mind. Untold memories cloud her thoughts.

Another figure joins the circle of people. Stepping out from the shadows of the room, he allows the light to reveal his sinister appearance. His long brown hair is tucked behind his ears, allowing full view of his face. The sharp shape of his nose and pointed chin are subtle in contrast to his yellow eyes. The eyes of a dragon. Dragon, as much a title as his name. He scans the onlookers and sneers.

A snatch into the air brings the flower into Dragon's hand. He holds it in a clasped fist, crushing the petals.

"Just kill him!" Dragon shouts, his voice gruff.

The Boss stands in shock, watching the petals fall to the floor. Rage builds up inside her. "Oh, Dragon," she says. "You shouldn't have done that."

Without another word from The Boss, Joe steps over to Dragon, gun in hand.

"Forget the flower," Dragon says. "We came here to do one thing, and—"

The crushing blow of Joe's pistol cuts Dragon off as it cracks hard into the side of his mouth. Dragon falls to the floor, knocking his now-broken teeth free.

His eyes strain to stay open. As he begins to lose consciousness, he hears a voice cry out.

"No!" It's Viper, calling for her fallen lover. She pushes past Joe, reaching out to Dragon.

Babu grabs her arm before she makes it to Dragon, holding her back with great force. Viper kicks and screams in a desperate rage, but she is overpowered. Babu drags her from the building.

"Take the girl and run," Babu grumbles, as he pushes Viper into the back of a large car. Her red hair sticks to her tear-soaked cheeks as she pleads to be let out, banging her fists on the window. Babu circles the rear of the car and lowers himself to the seat beside her.

The Boss storms into the garage, with Joe hobbling close behind. She's lost control. That loss will take its toll. The plan was simple at first: Kill Bullet. But now Dragon lies to the side of the enemy. So Joe and The Boss have chosen to retreat from the plan; a night like this would only have gotten worse.

"What's going on, Boss?" Joe asks, taking the driver's seat.

"Just drive, Joe," she demands.

In the warehouse, Dragon lies still, one eye filling with blood from an open wound. He wipes his red tears of pain away to survey the figure in front of him. It is Bullet, rising from the ground like a zombie from a fresh grave.

As Bullet moves toward the door after The Boss, he pushes his body to the limit. The reinforced joints of his suit click through cogs and gears. They wind a tension coil, and his next step thrusts forward. He reaches out his hand to open the door, but his fingers are powerless to press the lever.

He falls to his knees, still reaching for the handle of the door. His internal bleeding has taken him down. Bullet coughs, a splatter of blood spewing from his mouth. He turns to lean against the door, each breath increasingly clogged with fluid.

After a night on the streets of Freakland City, you either wake up to the lights of the hospital, or you're left in the darkness of the morgue.

CHAPTER 1

The hall lights of the hospital flickered—a generator power flux. Dr. Becker looked down at the young twin girls, each on a stretcher that rattled over the cracked concrete floor.

"I don't understand it. How could they both be infected?" the girls' father questioned, while trying to keep up with them.

The entire hospital team was panting through their masks; treating the infected came with extraordinary risk.

"Wait here! Your daughters are very sick." Dr. Becker spoke as clearly as he could through his mask.

The stretchers crashed through the double doors at the end of the corridor. *Do I have it?* The father touched the bare skin of his face. He stood in the emptiness of the hall, watching the swinging doors slow to a stop.

Two Guardian officers had come up behind him. One had restraints in hand; the other rested his hand on his firearm. Officer Marshall—The Preacher, they called him—let his thumb glide over the gun's safety.

"You need to come with us, Sam," said Marshall.

Sam turned to them. His face was already showing the effects of the virus. His eye caught a fire extinguisher, its glass case broken from frequent use. Sam grabbed the extinguisher from the wall and swung it around, slamming it into the nearest officer's mask. He fell to the floor.

"Stop!" Marshall shouted and drew his firearm. "Your family needs you."

Sam looked at Marshall's gun. The safety was still on. He reached down to pick up the pistol from the now-unconscious officer on the floor.

10

"Please, this doesn't have to be the end." Marshall's voice was throbbing.

Sam picked up the gun and turned toward the doors. Marshall's firearm was now pointed at him, but the father did not fear for his own life.

"Drop the gun!" Marshall hollered.

"In this world, you can't live with the safety on," Sam growled out. He spun around and fired the weapon. The bullet splintered the glass of Marshall's mask. Sam continued through the doorway as Marshall fell to the ground.

"What's happening?" Sam asked upon entering the emergency room.

"You need to get checked out. We're fine here." Becker didn't look up from young Jessica's ailing body.

"Fix them!" Sam waved the gun around at the mass of people in the room.

A metal tray of sanitized medical instruments crashed and slid across the concrete floor. A nurse reached down to pick up the tray, his eyes not leaving the flailing pistol. His deep exhale fogged his mask. He struggled to gather up the instruments, and the edge of a scalpel found his palm. The nurse jolted as his rubber glove ripped open and a trail of blood wet the torn edges. His chance of infection had just skyrocketed.

"We can't!" the nurse yelled out, bolting toward Sam with the scalpel in hand. His body stopped cold, as if he'd hit a brick wall in midair. A small whine whispered from his mouth, and he fell to the floor, dropping into a puddle of motionless limbs. Sam watched the small trail of smoke track from the tip of his hot pistol.

"Any other heroes?" He scowled at the eyes of Dr. Becker.

"This isn't the way to fix things," Becker replied.

"She's crashing!" said a nurse beside Jessica.

Next to her sister, Samantha was in a fever- driven nightmare, reliving what had happened earlier that day.

The two girls had planned on spending the afternoon playing at the park with their dad. Jessica picked up an old doll out of the rain gutter while waiting in line with her sister at the gate.

"Personal items stay here," the Guardian said.

Sam cringed at the sight of the doll, dirty and ratty. Even though they were all in the safety of their suits, he still feared infection from material things.

"You heard the man, Jess." Sam pointed to a large garbage can to the side of the gate.

The family entered through the first door. Large vacuums switched on and decontaminated the holding room. Now, along with two other families, they could remove their masks and enter the park.

Samantha ran over to the swings first thing. She closed her eyes as Sam pushed her higher and higher. The wind of the motion helped her to forget about the outside world. For a moment, she didn't think of the protective dome over the playground, only freedom.

"Hey, where's your sister?" Sam asked, looking about the area.

"I'll go find her," Samantha said, to keep her dad from growing further annoyed with Jessica.

She searched everywhere, but Jessica wasn't in any of the places the other kids were. Then, off at the edge of the park, she saw a large concrete tube in the sandpit. Samantha rolled her eyes, knowing her sister must be in there.

"Jess? Hey, Jess, Dad's looking for you," Samantha called out as she dropped to her knees to crawl into the large tunnel.

She found her sister unconscious with the doll grasped in her hands. Jessica had managed to sneak the doll through the holding room and into the clean site.

Samantha screamed for help. A wailing alarm sounded, and Guardians stormed the area. Panic spread, and chaos followed. People stormed the front gate, trampling over one another to reach the holding room.

Sam gave a statement to an officer while Jessica was loaded onto a stretcher. Samantha watched the medics treat her own twin as if she were already dead.

The sounds of sirens and screams still echoed through the enclosed area. Samantha grew very dizzy. She watched as the swing set turned sideways, and then her face hit the ground.

"Save Samantha!" Sam shot into the ceiling. The shot snapped Samantha out of her dream.

"Daddy?" Samantha was terrified of the scene before her.

"It's okay, baby, these doctors will fix you. Isn't that right?" Sam demanded as he turned toward Becker.

"Even if we could help them, it's only a matter of time before—" Becker stopped short.

"If she dies, you all die!" Sam nodded toward Samantha.

"What about Jess?" Samantha asked.

Sam lowered his voice. "You're the only thing that matters, honey. Everything will be okay."

The monitor showed that Jessica's heart rate had regulated. She had made it through the first phase. The remaining nurses pushed fluids and antibiotics.

"Wait. Start a transfusion," Becker said at a barely audible level.

"Excuse me, Doctor?" The nurse to his side was perplexed.

"Start a transfusion. I have an idea." Becker didn't blink; his *vision* focused on his thoughts.

The lead nurse confronted the doctor. "Please, Dr. Becker. You know they don't have a chance."

Becker flinched, trying to suppress a volcanic eruption of recollections. Guilt flooded his mind. "It's not my fault!"

Becker had emerged from his state of despondency. Still, the agony of the memories lingered.

Sam found it hard to remain on his feet. He lowered himself to the floor, leaning against the wall.

"One of these bullets has your name on it, Doc." Sam held the gun up. "Blame whoever you'd like for that."

Becker looked down at Sam. The threat may have been fading, but so were the lives of the young girls.

"The blood vessels in her brain have started to die," Becker noted, reviewing Jessica's monitor. "We need to locate the source of the infection before her organs shut down."

The doctor nodded to his staff to continue with Jessica. Approaching Samantha, he could not avoid her eyes. Her family was dying in front of her, but her eyes told a separate story. *She will survive.*

"Samantha will become the heir." Sam pushed the words from his blood-soaked lips. He was struggling to remain conscious. The virus was wearing him down.

"Samantha, is it?" Becker placed his hand on her shoulder. "Please lie back."

Samantha looked down at her father, then over to her sister, before allowing Becker's hand to guide her back down.

"He blames her for our mother's death," Samantha said, turning her head toward her sister once more.

Becker used his stethoscope to listen to Samantha's heart.

"I was born first. They didn't know I had a sister. Our mom died when Jess got stuck, but it wasn't her fault," Samantha continued, eyes welling with tears.

"Doctor, we have the results," the lead nurse interjected.

Becker reviewed the blood sample with apprehensive eagerness. "The blood makes its loop through the lungs, where it is oxygenated. The lungs are infected, so the blood then carries the virus throughout her bloodstream," he revealed.

There was little time to consider the troublesome findings; Samantha's heart monitor signaled a dramatic change.

"Her heart is infected," Becker announced. "We need to perform a transplant."

"Nobody leaves this room," Sam barked, coming to.

Becker nodded at Sam. "Her sister will be the donor."

The lead nurse continued pumping oxygen into Jessica's lungs. "Mathew, you can't mean that."

"We don't have a choice," Becker said in defense. "She will suffer a cardiac arrest at any moment."

Becker was neither young nor old. He had a few gray strands of hair, and his build told a story of health and determination. But his hands, his hands were those of an artist. That's what he was. Not of any common nature. He worked with the most delicate and complicated forums. The art of surgical precision.

The medical staff was numb. The stress and anxiety had exhausted them all. Still, they did as the doctor instructed. They worked carefully as he opened both girls' chests, before proceeding to clamp and then cut out Jessica's heart. In a vital time frame, the team worked together to place Jessica's heart into Samantha's chest.

"When she wakes up," Becker instructed his staff, "Samantha will need to be transferred to a special recovery unit to be rehabilitated. How long she remains in the hospital will depend

14

on her general health and how well the new heart is working. Once she's released, she will have to return to the hospital for regular check-ups and rehabilitation sessions. The number of visits to the hospital will decrease over time as she adjusts to her transplant. But Samantha will remain on immunosuppressive medication for the rest of her life to avoid the possibility of rejection."

Sam gazed up from the floor to his daughter; the image was his last.

Becker poured three fingers of scotch to refill his glass. He tipped the bottle toward his companion, Jane, offering it. She slid her glass to him in acceptance. "Do you know where Samantha is now?"

"She was placed in foster care until she came of age. I dread to think how she's survived since then." Becker smeared the drops of scotch from his bearded face and continued. "I did everything I could for her. We just need a better treatment option."

"But you've saved lives with organ transplants?" Jane questioned.

"The virus damages so many cells as the host becomes infected and the viral infection takes over. Removing the infected organ extends their life, but they're not cured."

"You're doing everything you can to help them," Jane said. "I remember being so scared when you told me I had breast cancer, but you helped me through it. Even after we left Chicago and came here, you looked after me. You're more than a doctor, Matthew Becker. You're a hero."

CHAPTER 2

The rainy season had lasted much longer than it had before the noxious clouds appeared. The short months of clear skies brought many from their shelter to the safe zone. Still, it was a cool afternoon for so late in the spring.

The weather didn't bother her. It never had. She shifted her weight and leaned against the lamppost. Waiting now, into the second hour, didn't bother her. The waiting was its own reward; it made the coming moment all the better. What did bother her was that she wasn't able to have a cigarette. She couldn't very well remove her mask. Not here, not while she was trying to blend in. *That wouldn't do. That wouldn't do at all.*

She ran her slim fingers down the front of her skirt, starting at the high waist and continuing down to her upper thigh. She could feel the outline of her cigarette case, tucked into the top of her long stockings. Tracing the outline over the coarse fabric felt . . . reassuring.

A group of clamorous children passed by. Even muffled by their masks, their shrill chatter was exasperating. It was as if each slowed to smile at her before entering the holding room of the park. Her mouth curled into an uncomfortable smile of her own. *Your life was over before it began.*

The loudspeaker blared the rules and restrictions for entering the park. Amused, she listened and tried to imagine which of the visitors wouldn't be paying attention. Which of these families would be surprised that their picnic blanket wouldn't be going inside. *Idiots!* With a quick swipe, she checked for her case again.

16

A putrid man was loitering across the street. He glanced at her with helpless eyes and moved on, looking for help elsewhere. A couple passed by him, appalled by the ailing man. The infected had become disregarded as the living dead. Effortless to ignore, hazardous to mingle with. The couple hurried across the street. *You're next!* she thought.

To pass the time, she imagined them choking on the toxic air. Oh, how they would scream in anguish. She giggled, but then she caught herself. Giggles weren't proper, not this afternoon. There would be time to laugh later.

She shifted off the post, her low heels pressing into the dirt beneath the grass. She wiggled her toes in the uncomfortable shoes. Couldn't let her feet fall asleep. That wouldn't do. Couldn't draw unnecessary attention to herself, either. *That would never do.* Not for something as silly as pinched toes. Besides, she had told herself these shoes would be fine.

The roundness of her broad butt was straining against the tight fabric of her skirt. It was worth it, she had convinced herself. She looked good. *I'm okay.* The buttons of her white shirt strained with the rise of her deep breath. *I'm fine.*

This was worth the trouble. She had to prove herself valuable. More valuable than the flesh each passing dog was eager to sniff. *Men are such an ugly race of animals.* She imagined them with tormented faces, in agony, pleading at her feet.

All at once, her fantasy ceased, and reality captured her full attention. He had finally arrived. Robert commanded attention. *Some people are better suited for the apocalypse.*

He was near now; it was time to move. The first step sent tingles up her calf. The hours of standing hadn't been kind to her restless body. Her ankle gave way, and she fell against him. Her face was pressed to his midsection. Slithering fingers crawled up his chest as she regained her balance. *Perfect.* She pushed off him.

"Pardon me, miss. Are you all right? You took a good spill there." Robert placed his large hands on her shoulders.

"Oh, yes, thank you. It's these darn shoes." She motioned toward her feet.

The two stood in line for access to the park. She rested her head on his bulging bicep; he was far too tall for her to reach his shoulder. His voice had grown tiresome to her. She was responding in little hums and nods by the time they reached the gate.

"Thank you for waiting with me." She looked up at him, putting on the best doe-eyed look she could manage.

"Of course. My pleasure." Robert's smile widened.

The vacuums decontaminated the holding room. The pair removed their masks and continued on. The sun seemed so much brighter inside. Combined with the radiant heat, it was almost like it would have been. She twirled and spun in the freedom of the area. Now it was time to giggle.

"I haven't been here since I was a little girl." She smiled down at the man, who was lying on the artificial grass.

She had been so patient. At last, the time had come. Reaching down to the hem of her shirt, she began to hike it up little by little.

"Oh no, miss. I'm sorry. You don't have to—" Robert reached for her hands to stop her.

She gave her skirt a quick tug and tore it to reveal her thigh, then pulled the cigarette case from her stocking and produced a match in short order. She took the first drag and watched his stupefied face pucker at the scent.

The unwell, diminutive man from the street outside watched through the glass of the dome. He remained at the edge of the enclosure, spitting vile slurs at the onlooking patrons. His mouth looked as if it could house maggots.

At last, he seemed content with his tinkering beneath his jacket. The explosive device he revealed from under his jacket was primitive in design. Still, it triggered an instant panic.

Noticing the commotion, the behemoth scrambled to his feet. He took several long strides toward the bomber. *Great, he thinks he's a hero.*

When the bomb exploded, the sound was deafening in the dome. The glass of the dome breaking was enough to trigger the reactions; she saw her fantasy realized. They all choked. They all panicked. *Idiots!* She hurried toward the big man, who was rolling across the ground, holding his head.

"Get up, dog," she demanded.

"Ba-boom, ba-boom," Robert kept repeating as he rocked from side to side.

"Hey, boss, is this the guy you wanted?" Joe, the bomber, asked, leaping over the injured people in his path.

"Joe, I told you not to set it off so close to us. You gave him a concussion."

"Ba-boom?" Robert tried to sit up.

"Yes, ba-boom. There was an explosion." She looked at Joe with wide eyes, signaling for him to help the larger man.

"Okay, Ba-boom, let's get you on your feet," Joe said, straining under the weight of the stunned man.

"Lawrence, please take a seat." The request came via the metal-clad faceplate. An amplifying speaker distorted the voice.

"There was an attack at the park. I can't tell you yet how many believe they were infected. Regardless of the findings, it was too many," Marshall began.

"I will send a crew out to evaluate the damage," Lawrence said, looking over the spread of paperwork on the desk between them.

"No, people need to understand the risk that comes with Old Town. I've issued a Guardian order to close the park."

"What about the zoo and the theater? You can't expect people to stop going; it's all that's left of normalcy." Lawrence's voice was laced with tension.

Marshall reached for his Guardian handbook. "'For I tell you, unless your righteousness exceeds that of the scribes and Pharisees, you will never enter the kingdom of heaven,'" he read.

"New Franklin isn't heaven, it's a mirage. The residents won't have a choice but to live the way you want them to. Where is your faith in humanity to make the right choice?"

"How dare you question my faith! I am a man of God. Only He can pass judgment. I am but a humble messenger. One who tells the truth of living in sin. Old Town will tarnish even the purest of men."

"Old Town was designed to give people hope. It wasn't about God, temptation, or anything you've attached to it."

"Maybe you've forgotten how much I've sacrificed."

Marshall pressed on either side of his faceplate; a puff of air hissed as he removed it. Lawrence was struck by what he saw. Marshall's dark skin and fatigued expression showed every passing year of demanding service. Lawrence focused on his right eye, or where it would have been. The terrible scar was jagged over the closed lid.

"The man who took my eye was said to be the last of his kind. He died in the hospital that night. I prayed that such evil would not return, but it has. Now, we must all make sacrifices."

"Save me the theatrics. We have already made sacrifices. Everyone here knows loss. You can't believe these people will leave their loved ones behind."

"When construction of New Franklin is complete, I have no doubt the pure will thrive under its protection. As for the infected, we need them to believe they have a chance."

"Those who have had transplants are still infected with the virus. What *chance* do they have?"

"That brings us to the reason I asked you here. We've reopened the FCRC. Doctor Ashland—"

"The geneticist?" Lawrence interrupted.

"Yes. Although his work, as of late, has been primarily focused on animals. He seems to think their immunity is the key to finding a cure."

"A cure? Is that what we're selling them on now?"

"As I said, we need them to believe they have a chance. Dr. Becker—"

"He's here? I know him. We went to med school together." Lawrence was eager to make the point.

"Your file says you dropped out."

"I was better suited to preventive measures."

"Right, so you joined the arms race."

"I designed tactical military gear for *defense*. You know this!" Lawrence slammed his hand down on the desk.

"Of course, and we appreciate all you've done to keep us safe in this." Marshall picked up his Guardian-issue faceplate. "I would've liked to have had this when I served."

"What do you want from me now?"

"I need you and Dr. Becker to assist at the research center."

"I'll see if he's interested."

"See to it that he is. That's an order."

20

CHAPTER 3

Long past were the days of cinematic monsters striking fear into uneasy moviegoers. The horror of reality left little room for imagination. Still, he would have sworn the man pounding on the door was out of a forgotten nightmare.

He sat up with a jolt, trying to recall how he'd landed in such an unsightly room. The pounding at the door knocked the memory loose from captivity. He was at Veronica's place. She stirred beside him.

The pounding continued. "I know you're in there, damn it. Open the door!"

The anxious man reached for the bedding and covered himself to his chin. A variety of classic horror monsters surged through his frantic mind like a Rolodex. The gloom of the room and a lingering buzz made his imagination vivid. *Not altogether helpful,* he thought, and asked about the monster's identity instead.

"Is that your husband?" He sniffled.

Veronica lifted her head from the pillow and then held it over her face. "I don't know which of you is more annoying right now, but I need my beauty sleep!" She groaned from under the pillow.

He didn't give much thought to the fire escape. If he opened the seal of the window, he'd reveal more than he had in his drunken ramblings earlier. He paused. Had he told her he was infected? *No, she wouldn't have slept with me.* All the precautions she took getting cleaned off before they went to bed. *My secret must be safe.*

"Veronica, don't listen to him. He's infected!"

The door cracked open, but the true monster was already inside.

"What did he say?" Veronica was awake and sitting upright.

"I said, he's infected." Her husband stood in the bedroom doorway. The light of the living room behind cast him in silhouette.

The petrified man looked like a cornered weasel, crying out for help as the hen's eggs lay scattered. The weasel stood from the bed. His naked body revealed the virus was attacking his skin. With each passing moment, he became more aware of the changes to his body. His fatty tissues were rapidly dissolving; ashen skin was shriveling tight to his body, and his veins bulged with black blood.

"Get him out of here, Drake!" Veronica yelled to her husband.

Drake charged forward, driving into the sick man. The infection left him weak, powerless to block the blow. Regardless, he would have let himself be smashed through the window. The instant where he could have attempted to catch the railing of the fire escape passed. As did each floor of the building.

Drake looked out from the window, down to the blood-splattered sidewalk below. He shifted back to Veronica, who was quivering under the tightly wrapped blanket. He slid into bed beside her. The breath from the window was a continuous expression of his vulnerability to the virus. Worse yet, if Veronica was infected, she would be contagious.

Veronica nestled against his chest. She unbuttoned his pants and advanced with wandering fingers.

The arrival of the brothel-keeper, Miles, and his rowdies didn't slow the lovers.

"You freaks!" he yelled through his mask. "You'll have the whole building condemned!" He stormed from the bed to the open window. "Look what you've done."

Drake grabbed his trousers as he climbed from the bed. Veronica wrapped herself with the blanket.

"Get them out of here!" Miles motioned toward them in disgust.

The couple was shoved out the side exit of the building, into an alleyway. At the opening of the alley, Veronica turned and saw the marquee of the neighboring theater.

"We've never been," she stated, eyeing Drake. He stared into her passionate eyes, but she broke away. "It's starting." Veronica's senses were waning, her words slurred.

Drake held her at his side as they trudged down the roadway.

"Do you think Miles was right? Did we put their lives at risk?" Veronica asked, straining to get the words out.

"All the girls knew the risk."

"What about the Johns?"

"What about them?"

"They traded some pretty valuable things for the opportunity —" Veronica's breath ran short.

"More valuable than your life?" Drake asked, turning Veronica to look her in the face. He glanced past her to see the frightened inhabitants of the city's dawn were fleeing from the two of them.

"You're showing signs of infection. We need to get off the streets," Drake said, guiding Veronica.

"I won't make it to the hospital."

"We aren't going to the hospital." Drake scooped Veronica off her feet and carried her.

The building was unnamed but designated with a yellow neon cross. *Yellow means research*. Drake was certain he'd found the correct place. He struggled to reach the handle of the entry door; it was impossible while holding Veronica.

"I can stand," she said, lowering her legs from his hold.

The lobby was raw. Chipped marble floors reflected the dismal desolation of the space. Blue- cushioned chairs lined the walls on either side of the entry.

"You're in the right place," said a voice over the intercom.

Drake looked to the window opposite the entrance. He connected the voice to the young woman seated at the window. She offered a thin smile, rounded off with freckled cheeks. *A trustworthy face,* Drake concluded.

"Thank you for choosing Franklin City Research Center. My name is Heather. What brings you in today?" the receptionist greeted them.

"Is she for real?" Veronica asked with hollow breaths.

"Listen, Heather, I appreciate the charm and all, but we've got ourselves into a real mess here. Is there a doctor available? She needs to be seen right away." Drake was struggling to keep Veronica upright as he spoke.

"A doctor? Why, yes, Dr. Ashland is in. I have to ask you, though, do you understand what we do here?"

"I've heard of this place. You can fix people up so they look normal again. And my lady here needs her looks."

"I see. Well, the good news is, we have room for you. But there are a few questions first. *One:* which animal best fits your temperament?"

"Animal?" Veronica asked.

A slender young woman crossed in front of the building. She was careful not to catch her heels on the broken sidewalk. Her red jacket, splattered with drops of rain, was growing heavy on her shoulders. Rhian paused and stared at the yellow neon cross. *What else can I do?* She entered the research center.

Rhian expected white-coated scientists moving in silent concession, studying samples under microscopes and transferring fluids from tube to tube. Instead, she stood in the cold lobby. Beyond the window to the front office, a vacant chair offered no explanation. She turned away to exit.

"Where will you go?" a soft voice whispered in the chill of the room.

"Oh! I didn't see you there," Rhian replied, noticing the frail woman sitting to the side of the door.

"Where will you go, to escape your fate?" The woman's trembling hand reached for Rhian's.

Rhian met the handshake. The woman's fingers were so slender it seemed like only skin and bone remained.

"I'm Lori, Lori Mouser," the woman introduced herself. Her hand fell limply from Rhian's grasp. Lori's head rocked forward, and Rhian could see where clusters of her coiled black hair had fallen out.

24

"I'm Rhian, um, Feist. Listen, are you going to be okay? You don't look so good." Rhian took a seat.

"Your accent is lovely. Where are you from?" Lori leaned her head back on the chair, drawing deep breaths as she spoke.

"England," Rhian responded simply. "Have you been waiting long? Is there anything I can do?"

"Lori Mouser," Heather called through the intercom. "The doctor will see you now." "Here, let me help you." Rhian took Lori's arm.

"You don't have long, dear." Lori broke free from Rhian and proceeded alone.

Rhian stood in the center of the room. A buzzer sounded, and a light above the interior door glowed green. Lori pulled open the door to enter. Rhian shifted her head to see what was inside. She caught only a glimpse of a man in a white lab coat.

"Excuse me, miss, may I help you?" Heather asked.

"I was an actress before . . . well, before this." Rhian stared at her open hands; the infection had started. "People don't want to see us, the infected; we're already dead to them. This is my only chance to be normal, the only way I can go back."

Heather nodded. "Okay, then I just have a few questions."

"It's good to see you again, old friend." Lawrence placed one hand on Dr. Becker's shoulder and, with the other, gave him a firm handshake.

"Yes, Lawrence, it's nice to see you made it through all of this," Becker said through his mask. He scanned the lobby of the research center, waiting for the signal indicating it was time to move on.

"Hey, we ain't through it yet, buddy." Lawrence pointed to his mask.

The buzzer sounded in the room. The door from the lobby unlocked.

"Ms. Cove." Lawrence nodded to Heather.

"Mr. Williams," Heather replied. Her cheeks hurt from smiling for so long. *Just keep smiling.* If the corners of her lips fell, she may reveal her true feelings. She strained to keep her composure until the men were gone.

"Surgical procedure room." Lawrence paused and opened a single door off the main hall.

Becker saw a familiar space: pure, disease-free, with glareless light beaming down on a draped operating table. Becker looked back at Lawrence, who had continued down the hall.

"What is it you're doing here?" Becker hollered.

"There's someone I want you to meet." Lawrence waited at the end of the hall.

Becker followed Lawrence through a narrow doorway. Animal cages of various sizes were placed around the room. At first glance, Becker wasn't sure the animals were alive. He took a slow breath through his mask, grateful he couldn't smell.

"I thought you said this was a genetics lab," Becker said.

"Just give me a minute to explain," said Lawrence in defense.

The clatter of a typewriter was faint but present, a sound Becker heard more with each passing year—he wrote his own chart notes this way. It meant they were not alone in the room, Becker realized.

"Ash, let me introduce you to a good friend of mine, Dr. Matthew Becker," said Lawrence.

"Why did you call him *Ash*?"

"Because that's his name, Matt. That, and—" Lawrence stopped short as Ashland stepped out from behind a wolf cage.

Becker kept his focus on the animal within. The wolf dropped to the floor of the cage. It was as though he meant to lie down but gave up along the way. His large gray head rested on his paws. The wolf's claws were unlike that of a pet dog. They hadn't been clipped; rather, they were filed by wear and tear.

The approaching man could be avoided no longer. Becker looked at Ashland. He was a short, frail man. For a moment, Becker, at fifty, felt like the younger man. But it wasn't Ashland's age that struck him. It was his skin. *Gray and white . . . Ash.* Becker understood the name now. *It's as though his skin structure has broken down in some way.*

"This is Dr. Ben Ashland," said Lawrence, realizing his previous introduction had been one-sided.

"Ah, the good doctor." Ashland sneered.

26

Lawrence stroked the length of his tie. The body language of the pair before him left little room for doubt about their feelings for one another. He decided that he would play his hand anyway.

"I've brought you together to discuss the future of medical treatment," Lawrence began.

"I told you already, I'm not in need of a surgeon," Ashland said dismissively.

"Becker is much more than that. His findings from the operation he performed were nothing short of genius," Lawrence proclaimed.

"Although the outcome with the second child was unfortunate," Becker interjected.

"Most unfortunate, and unnecessary." Ashland placed his hand on the wolf cage.

"In clinical trials, Dr. Ash has eradicated the virus from a human DNA strand," said Lawrence, trying to keep the conversation afloat.

"There is a cure," Dr. Ashland said, straining for the words, his voice only just above a whisper.

"A cure? I believe you mean a vaccine. Poxta is a nuclear-weaponized varicella-zoster virus," Becker retorted.

Ashland drew his hands quickly to his face as he began to cough.

Becker took the moment to explain. "He would have to develop an attenuated live strain of the Poxta virus that would stimulate the immune system but not cause disease. Even then, the vaccinated could be contagious."

Ashland's coughing eased in intensity, until he regained his slow, shallow breaths.

"It's not a vaccine. The broken strand can be repaired." Ashland's lips dripped with blood as he spoke.

"Ash has developed a drug that pushes the transcription process," Lawrence added. "By copying a DNA sequence, he can make an RNA molecule, which can then be spliced and copied to repair all damaged cells."

Becker nodded at Ashland. "I assume your suffering comes from your trials to accomplish this horrific fantasy?"

"I discovered there are *some* things worse than death." Ash's voice was soft as he avoided straining his throat. He turned away as he wiped the drying blood from his mouth.

"He removed the infected cells. What you see is all that remains," Lawrence mumbled.

Becker shrugged. "I have patients to attend to."

"They won't need organ transplants, not with the immunity from animal DNA."

"You're copying a sequence from these animals?"

"Yeah, Matt, that's what I've been trying to show you." Lawrence motioned to the cages.

Everything made sense now. *Dr. Ashland's condition. His motivation. And these animals*. Still, Becker was missing one vital piece. *What do they want from me?*

"You've come on an important day, Dr. Becker." Ashland tucked his blood-stained handkerchief into his lab coat pocket.

"That's right, we're assigning animals to patients today," Lawrence chimed in.

"There are patients here?" Becker was outraged.

"Strictly volunteers, I assure you." Lawrence waved his hands in defense.

"*Patient name: Wallace Hunter. Exposure: two days. Animal: wolf*," Ashland recited from his prepared list.

"Two days? What is his treatment plan?" Becker approached Ashland to view the report.

Lawrence played the final card of his hand. "That's why you're here. We begin human trials tomorrow. Think you can make sure he lives that long?"

———————————————

"Easy, baby. You're okay. That's it." Lori removed the tangled barbed wire from the cat's rear paw. It limped for a moment before lying down.

"That thing gonna be ready for transport by morning?" a voice called out. Lori spun around, looking up to the terrace above the enclosure.

"She's frightened. Give me time to calm her down. I need to dress her wounds."

"A few scratches won't keep them from taking her, Lori. Best you say your goodbyes now."

28

Lori frowned. Her favorite animal, the lynx, would be gone in the morning. It was no use denying it. They had taken a dozen small animals already.

Everyone had made their rounds, gawking at the animals. It was late now, and the zoo was closed.

Lori looked at the sky. The rain cascaded over the dome as if it were a large umbrella. She bowed her head, locked her office door, and headed for the exit.

"Travis, I don't care how many there are—grab their stupid ears and put them in the cage," Lori heard the man yelling. *They're not supposed to be here until the morning.* Lori hurried down the path toward the sound.

"Hey, Donny, if I get sick, I hope they use rabbit blood on me. I'd enjoy the extra stamina."

"You're an idiot, Trav. Hurry up, we still need to get the cat."

Lori's eyes widened. She backed away from the men. *They can't take her.*

"Come here, girl." It was dark in the cage; Lori stumbled, searching for the cat. "Don't be afraid."

At last, she found her. "Okay, you have to trust me." Lori removed her jacket and draped it over the cat. The lynx was young, nowhere near full grown. Still, Lori struggled to keep her under the jacket while she ran toward the exit.

"Hey! Do you work here? Where are you off to in such a hurry?" Travis stood near the exit, holding a crate overstuffed with rabbits.

"Stop her! She has the cat!" Donny was rounding the corner.

Lori grabbed a mask from the security kiosk, burst through the holding room door, and plunged her key into the switch for the decontamination to cycle.

"I'm sorry, baby, you're not going to like this." She held on to the cat tightly as the air circulated in the holding room.

The outer door opened. Lori dropped to her knees.

"Okay. Go on, girl. Run!" Lori flapped her jacket at the cat.

The lynx froze with fright, looking out into the night, and then back at Lori. She heard the holding room cycle again behind her.

"It's okay, it's me. See? It's okay. Don't be afraid." Lori lowered her mask.

"Don't be stupid!" Donny was behind her, surrounding her body with his. He reached down and replaced her mask.

While Lori jerked to get away, she watched, petrified, as Travis seized the cat.

Lori jolted awake. *No!* She sat up in her cot. A candle was still glowing at her bedside. Across the room, in a cage, Lori could just make out the faint glow of the lynx's eyes.

She hadn't the strength to reach the cage. She couldn't attempt to free her. *I'm sorry.* Lori collapsed onto her back, face twisted in agony.

Wallace had awoken too. "What is it?" he asked.

"That's my friend." Lori pointed.

"The cat? I got my animal too. I think we all did." Wallace tried to roll over to face Lori, but he only managed to lift his arm. His dark skin was barely visible in the flickering light. He closed his fist. Weakness shrouded his anger as he relaxed his hand.

"Feeling any better?" Lori asked.

"Doc said maybe by morning."

"Do you trust him?"

"Becker?"

"Yes. Do you think he can help us?" Lori struggled to stay awake.

"He made us this drip cocktail." Wallace looked at his intravenous therapy.

"I could really go for a Bloody Mary right now."

"You and me both, sister."

CHAPTER 4

The Boss, as they had come to call her, surrounded herself with self-indulgence. She sat in the high-backed leather chair, feet perched on the lip of the walnut desk. The Boss flicked the ash from her cigarette and let out a stream of smoke.

She lowered her feet, leaned into the desk, and looked down at the man on the floor, who was pleading desperately for his life. The hypnotic swirls of the travertine floor seemed to ripple in the surrounding candlelight.

"Please, I've done what you asked. Spare my life!" he cried out.

His knees ached as he shifted from one to the other. His red face was smeared with tears and snot. Nothing was so pitiful as a man facing injustice.

He had killed someone, taken their organs, just to save Robert. A man who could not even remember his real name. Because *she* said he was more important. The doctor had done what she asked, and yet, the muzzle of Joe's pistol pressed all the harder into his head.

The Boss pulled a rose from the bouquet on her desk. She leaned back in her chair and began pulling petals from the flower. *We kill him, we kill him not.* She smiled at her captive.

"Joe and Robert are only the beginning. I need an army," The Boss said, dropping the final petal to the floor.

A flash of white light filled the room. The lightning penetrated the darkness. Thunder followed closely, rattling the glasses on the adjacent bar.

Sweat began to build on the doctor's brow as he went pale. Nausea clawed at his throat. He tried to force down the bile, but his nerves pushed over the limit, and he spewed vomit onto the floor.

"Just kill me," he said in surrender.

The Boss shook her head at Joe. He withdrew his weapon.

"But, Dr. Kranes, if I killed you, who would take care of your wife?" she asked.

Kranes's life had been spared years ago. Dr. Becker had found him a suitable donor. He understood that his life was important. He could go on to save many others. If his wife got sick, would Becker show the same mercy? *I would do anything to save her. Anything!* Kranes pushed himself upright and rose to his feet.

"Okay. I'll do it. Whatever you want. Just, please, leave her out of this."

The Boss always took two olives in her martini. Tonight was no different. She dumped them into her glass. She paid no attention to them until the drink was little more than a spoonful in the glass. She rotated the glass in small circles, driving the olives in a race around the rim. The effortless motion of her wrist sent them spiraling in a seemingly endless pursuit. Finally, she tired of the game and poured the contents into the waste bin.

"Men today, you just don't have the balls. Joe, take Dr. Kranes back to his lab. Then I want you and Robert to find me some more organ donors. We have a lot of work to do."

"Sure, Boss, we're on it. Come on, Babu," Joe said, beckoning for Robert to follow.

"What did you call him?" The Boss asked.

"I've been trying to teach him his name again. Robert wasn't happening. Tried Bobby. The most I can get out of this big dummy is *Babu*."

The Boss shook her head and pulled a cigarette from her case. "Have fun, boys."

Lucy stood in the holding room of The Red Tent. She held down her dress as the blasts of air cycled through. The tired breaths in her mask served as a reminder of the dangers outside.

The dangers of leaving were vast, but too many women had become infected for her to continue working.

It struck her that it had been many months since she had been outside. All the nights of *their* pleasure amounted to a single suppressed memory. *A nightmare.* The street looked different from the view she had from her window. *Bigger. Darker.*

The sounds from outside the theater echoed off the buildings. The laughter and banter was distorted by people's masks. *They sound like hyenas.* Lucy feared she would be recognized by her clientele and headed away.

Her mind presented visual aids for her fears. *I want to wash my brain in cold water.* Lucy stopped and slid her shoes off. Her heels offered little support on the rough terrain of the desolate street.

"You should have stayed inside. It's not safe out here." The voice came from behind her. Eager footsteps approached.

Lucy felt her heart begin to pound in her chest. She darted across the street toward the courthouse. Frantically, she climbed the stairs to the entrance.

The floor inside was slippery. The damaged roof had allowed rain to flood the building. Lucy regretted discarding her shoes as she slipped and fell. Her ankle throbbed, but she only remained down for a moment. He was closing in; she could hear his footsteps on the cracked marble floor.

Panic-ridden, labored breath fogging her mask, Lucy saw the man—a ghoulish half-pint—round the corner. She turned to flee, but she ran into a behemoth.

"Please, you have to help me. He's trying to kill me," the woman pleaded with the human barrier.

"Grab her, you fool," said Joe. "Don't let her get away."

Babu closed his arms around the petite woman. Weariness overcame her, and her struggles were weak as she began to sob.

"Sorry, lady." Babu lifted her to carry her back outside.

Joe bared his rotten teeth at Lucy as Babu loaded her into the trunk like a sack of potatoes.

"Shame the pretty ones always get cut up for parts," said Joe.

The juvenile lay still, nervously awaiting the prick of the needle. He looked at his arm; it was stained with iodine. The band was tight around his bicep. Squeezing his fist tighter, he watched the blue veins inside his elbow swell.

His eyes shifted away from his arm, and he followed the doctor's movements. Dr. Kranes approached with the syringe. "Keep making a fist," he instructed.

When the vial was full of blood, the doctor removed the needle from the young man's arm. A small bit of gauze was placed over the puncture.

Kranes drained the blood into a test tube. He shook it and held it up to the light of the room. He took a seat at the desk opposite the anxious patient and dabbed two drops of blood onto a small, square piece of glass, which he then sandwiched between two glass slides. He switched on the light box of the microscope and placed the sample on it before beginning to adjust the lens.

"How long until we'll have the results?"

The doctor lifted his straining eyes from the microscope and turned to answer the question. His face revealed the truth, and his voice fell to an inaudible murmur as the young man's fears were realized.

"But I don't feel sick." His words bubbled out of his weeping face.

The doctor rose from the chair and stepped to the door of the makeshift medical room. "I understand this is devastating news. I will give you some time alone."

The doctor closed the door behind him, then paused as he heard the cries of the boy.

"He's infected. Given the dramatic loss in white blood cells, I'm guessing he has two, maybe three days before an organ transplant would be futile," Kranes explained quietly to The Boss outside the door.

"You let me worry about finding a donor, Dr. Kranes. You just be ready to do your job."

"Thomas, is it?" The Boss looked up from the chart as she entered the room.

"Yes, ma'am," Thomas answered, wiping snot from his nose.

"I'm very sorry to hear about your test results. Do you know how you may have been exposed?"

"I was just leaving The Red Tent when Dr. Kranes approached me. He told me some of the girls there were infected and that I should get checked out." Explained Thomas.

"Forgive me. The Red Tent?"

"It's a building in Old Town by the theater. They call it The Red Tent because all the plastic sheeting over the windows is tinted red."

"All right, Thomas, I want to help you. There's just the issue of payment. How do you feel about changing employers?"

CHAPTER 5

"This blows!" Rhian lay on her cot, tapping her foot on the end bar.

"It's not the end of the world," Veronica teased with a faint smile.

"Ha! I see what you did there." Rhian turned her head toward her roommate.

Even as Veronica's life faded from her, Rhian thought she was stunning. *They should have beauty pageants for corpses.* Her crimson hair remained vibrant. The green in her eyes sparkled like emeralds.

"Do you know why I'm excited for today?" Rhian prompted.

Veronica rolled her eyes, "Not yet."

"Because if we survive, I have another erotic bedtime story to look forward to."

Veronica closed her eyes and smiled. *How embarrassing.* She had at least ten years on her. *Maybe I should have left some details out?* She turned her head to Rhian.

"How'd you get yourself into this mess, anyway?"

"Do you know the theater in Old Town?" Rhian began.

"I do," Veronica answered.

She knew it very well. Months had turned into years as her clientele staggered from the theater to her chambers. The brothel, like the theater, was a sealed building. You could remove your mask and breathe in the purified air. *You can't do that outside.* Both businesses offered spirits and cigars. The only real difference was, when a performer left the stage, they were gone. *The end.*

When Veronica stepped off the stage, the performance had just begun. *Then it started.*

"I went to my dressing room after the show. There were flowers left for me." Rhian wiped at her welling eyes.

"The card said, *Get well soon—Joe.*" Rhian sniffed and cleared her throat. "When my fever started, I understood what he meant."

Men wanted what they couldn't have. Veronica had known many Joes in her lifetime. She was grateful to have had Drake through it all. *I miss you.* He had always kept her safe.

"Did I tell you what happened to the man who did this to me? My husband pushed him out the window. There's probably still blood in the gutter."

"Your husband knew what you did, like, for work?"

"Yes, dear," said Veronica. "He even infected himself to be here with me."

"Rhian Feist. Veronica Casper," Dr. Becker read from a chart as he entered the room.

"Please, Doctor, when can I see my husband?"

"Oh." Becker reviewed the chart. "Yes, here, Drake Casper. I see your exposure times differ by at least eight hours. Is that right?"

"Yes, but we were separated, and—"

Becker held his hand up to signal Veronica to stop. "There are some things we still don't understand about the virus. As a precaution, you have been separated by the virus incubation period," he explained.

"Does that mean *we* were both infected at the same time?" Rhian asked.

"Based on the information you gave, yes."

Becker rolled the crash cart into the room and slid the glass door closed behind him. He tried to ignore the animals in the room. His plan of care did not include a snake or a rabbit. Yet, the pairing of such animals with these young women gave him pause for thought. He had reviewed their charts. *A snake and a rabbit?* Becker pushed past the question.

"I have medicine for you both. It will replace your current IV treatment."

Becker finished with what little he could do for them. As he closed the door behind him, he looked back into the room.

"Good luck." His words were meant to go unheard.

Ashland looked up from his chart as he approached Becker in the hall.

"Dr. Becker, how good of you to join us today," Ashland said with a sneer.

Becker begrudgingly held out his hand for a formal greeting. "Thank you. I'm curious, why the different animals?"

Ashland ignored the gesture and turned toward the glass door.

"That was all Lawrence. He said the subjects needed to be able to bond—" Ashland stopped to clear his throat.

Becker stood by the doorway as Ashland was faced with an exhausting effort to clear his lungs. In his admission of defeat, Ash resolved to take slow, shallow breaths.

"They feel a *connection* with their animal," he finally managed as he wheezed.

Lawrence began to describe to Wallace what he would experience during the procedure. "Wallace, you will be awake for this procedure. The injection will go into your neck. The needle will proceed between your sixth and seventh vertebrae and inject medication into your vertebral artery."

Becker stood numb, fixated by Wallace's monitor. *There are some things worse than death.* He repeated Ashland's words in his mind. Was this a better option than organ transplants? Becker found himself needing the answer.

"What will happen next," Lawrence continued, "is the antibody will travel to the subclavian artery branch. We have included a drug that will alter your brain's response, so that it immediately sends a signal to repair your DNA structure."

Wallace lay on the table in a pale blue hospital gown. His hands and feet tingled; the restraints were cutting off his circulation. He looked at the pair of doctors standing over him, each masked. The odor of his putrescent flesh was his alone to endure. *A masquerade.* Wallace saw through it all.

"I haven't got all day," he said bitterly.

38

Dr. Ashland entered the room. He held a metal tray; on it, a vial and syringe. The sounds in the room were clear. Filling the syringe barrel. Pressing the plunger to clear any trapped air. The pop of releasing latex gloves over spread fingertips. Then came the grinding of Wallace's teeth as he bore the painful injection. Finally, silence took over the room, revealing the echo of worry left behind.

Wallace was panting through his nose. His eyes were wide open. Dr. Becker shifted between patient and monitor. He shined his light into Wallace's eyes to check brain function. His pupils remained dilated.

"Can you hear me, Wallace? Concentrate on your breathing. In through your nose, out through your mouth."

Dr. Ashland leaned over Wallace. He placed his hand on the man's forehead and looked into his eyes. "Take note of the reflection in his eyes, Dr. Becker. You're looking at the development of tapetum lucidum."

"What does that mean?" Lawrence asked.

"It's a retroreflector. It reflects visible light back through the retina, increasing the light available to the photoreceptors. But it's impossible." Becker looked again with his light.

"It is possible." Ashland turned away to cough. "Some mutation is to be expected."

Lawrence looked at Wallace. "I don't think he's with us."

"Wallace?" Becker snapped his fingers.

The entire process of saving lives was a symphony. At times it was quiet. Becker was aware of the rise to a crescendo where the orchestra would burst. This awareness offered a chance to be the conductor. Wallace's heart rate raced on the monitor.

"Prep the defibrillator!"

Wallace felt as though the wolf was tearing his heart from his chest. It would take everything out of him, leaving only worthless scraps behind. *Get back, beast!* Wallace knew he had to fight it.

He shot up from his rested position. The bands on his ankles and wrists halted the motion. "Leave me alone!" he screamed, falling back on the table.

His entire body shook with uncontrollable muscle spasms. He twisted and turned, pulling the bands taut. Wallace growled through clenched teeth. Blood and saliva began to gather around his mouth.

The music stopped.

"Clear!" Becker placed the paddles on his chest. The room went dark. The monitor switched off.

"It's the generator. I'll go!" Lawrence shouted.

"Wait." Becker felt for a pulse. "He's alive." Becker switched on his flashlight. The second movement of the symphony was slower than the first. Becker, like the others, could only observe. Wallace's skin seemed to rejuvenate with each pulse. The damaged cells were healing.

Becker placed his stethoscope on Wallace's chest. "His vitals have improved, and his lungs are clear. I'll need to draw blood for testing, but I believe it's actually working."

Lawrence smiled. *They'll believe they have a chance now.*

"Hold the light still," Lawrence demanded of Becker.

"Jane will be worried about me." Becker aimed his flashlight back toward the generator.

Lawrence pulled his watch out. "I'll have you home in time for dinner."

Hot oil dripped from the motor onto Lawrence's mask.

"Can you imagine a day when we won't need these?" Lawrence asked, smearing the oil from the mask.

"Lawrence, I want to thank you."

"Hold that thought. I think I got it." The generator sputtered.

Lori awoke to the strobe of the overhead fluorescents turning back on. As they settled, her nerves did not. Dr. Ashland stood at her door with a metal tray in his hands.

"I know you sacrificed a lot to be with your cat. I want to make sure you're never apart again."

Ashland looked from Lori to the lynx.

Drake woke from a nightmare. His fever plagued his thoughts. The virus had caught up to him. *Veronica?* The echo of the dream remained. *Wait, there it is again.* Drake strained to hear. Her scream was faint but haunting in the halls of midnight.

Drake sat up in the bed and turned to lower his feet. He hadn't the strength to stand and tumbled to the floor. He rubbed at his sore arm, which had taken the brunt of the fall. The friction of the gesture tore open the fluid-filled blisters that had formed. Drake rolled onto his back to look at his arms and saw that the virus had spread overnight.

It wouldn't be long now. Cellular degradation would follow. *Veronica is dying and I'll soon follow.* Drake watched the flickering candle cast dancing shadows about the room. *I'll see you in hell, babe.* The thought of being together brought a smile to his face. He began to chuckle, then broke into maniacal laughter.

Drake couldn't hear the door to his room open over his outrageous episode. Tears streaming down his face, he alternated between yelling obscenities, laughing, and sobbing.

"Drake, get a hold of yourself," Ashland pleaded.

"What did you do to her, you son of a bitch?" Drake turned to see the faint glow of the lab coat in the doorway.

"Like the others, I have given her the cure. You are the last one."

"Liar! I heard her screams."

"It's a very painful shot, you see." Ashland set the metal tray on the cot and lifted the syringe. He held it above Drake on the floor.

"Now please, roll over. I need to put this in your neck."

"Do your worst."

Ashland began to administer the shot.

Drake's screams were not from the physical pain of the injection, but cries for truth. *Is it true?* He had to find out.

An unsettling commotion woke Wallace. The question of what waited to be discovered outside the room faded. Something was wrong with him.

His eyes opened to see no light, leaving his mind in darkness. He felt hunger, as if he had never eaten a day before in his life. The air was cold in his lungs, but his naked body was warm in the emptiness of the room.

What have they done to me? Am I cured now? I feel so different. I need to see myself. What is the blindfold protecting me from?

His hands were still in restraints. He pulled to full tension; the leather bands tightened over his wrists. He hadn't been able to break free since they put him in this room. Yet he pressed on, feeling his body growing stronger. A sudden rage came over him, a frantic obsession to be free. Finally, it happened—first his right hand, then his left.

All I want is to see my body; nothing feels right anymore.

He swiped at his face to remove the blindfold, finding it nearly impossible to use his fingers. There were bursts of pain across his eyes as the band came free. Blood distorted his vision— *my own blood, caused by my own hands. My hands? No, these claws can't be mine!*

He wiped his eyes to clear his vision. But nothing was clear; his body was no longer his own. He gave in to his agony with fearful howling.

Dr. Ashland dropped the tray. *What was that sound?* Leaving Drake unconscious on the floor, he quickly hobbled away, down the hall. He passed Veronica and Rhian. *Still asleep.* He glanced into Lori's room; she stirred in the bed. *Wallace?* Ashland began walking toward the lab.

Lori opened her eyes. Her elliptically shaped pupils adjusted to the dim light in the room.

Ashland fell onto the door of the lab, fighting to breathe. His cough sent blood splattering onto the portal window in the door. He removed his handkerchief and smeared the glass to a translucent red. *Your blindfold!* He could see Wallace inside.

Entering the room without fear, Ashland spoke gently. "I'm sorry I wasn't here to help you."

Wallace couldn't make out Ashland's words. Another voice overpowered them. *You're not a man anymore.* Free of his restraints, he slid from the table. *I have taken that from you.* Wallace stepped toward Ashland. *Eaten your very soul.* He bared his teeth. *And now I am hungry for more!*

Lori rounded the corner of the hall. The lab door was just ahead. Suddenly, the door broke free from the jamb and crashed into the hall. Amid the rubble of the broken door, Dr. Ashland lay motionless, his lab coat stained red with blood.

Then she saw him. She was frozen. Not by fear, but in awe of him. He stood in the passageway. Wallace caught her gaze. Their eyes locked on one another.

Abruptly, Wallace stumbled. His knees buckled under the stress. Lori sprang forward, trying to catch him as he fell to the floor. The two collapsed together. Lori felt his heart racing.

You're okay. Take it easy. Lori reached out to his long face as she tried to comfort him. Wallace snapped at her clawed fingers as they slid through the thin fur on his face. Lori retracted her hand quickly, but she felt his arms holding her still.

We have to find a place to hide. We won't be safe here. Not after this. Lori looked to Ashland's body and back to Wallace. He seemed to understand and released his hold.

Lori ran quickly into the night. Soon, she faded into the darkness. Wallace lost sight of her. He sprinted several strides after her. The pavement seemed to slide away under him. His knees were pumping too high. He tried to correct his stride by running even faster, until the street was a blur beneath him. Falling forward, he caught himself with outstretched arms. Running on all fours, it felt as though the ground formed into sections. Each leap forward promised the next awaiting piece.

CHAPTER 6

Jane knocked on Becker's door. She tried the handle. It was unlocked.

"Can I come in?" Jane called as she stepped softly into the room.

The dim light of the bedside lamp brought forth the flaws in Becker's aging face. There was something bruised about him, a constant pain beneath the surface. Becker sat up in the bed and pushed his pillow back against the headboard.

"What is it? Are you okay?" His eyes were dark and clouded, as if he was just about to fall asleep.

"Why were you late tonight?" Jane crossed her arms over her chest.

Becker could hear the anger in her voice. He didn't want to play to it, but avoiding it would be worse. He couldn't lie to her either.

"My father kept families together. I feel like all I've done is tear them apart," Becker said with despair.

"That's not true," Jane said. "You've done so much to help them."

"But what if I didn't do the right thing?"

Jane stepped to the bedside and began to caress his shoulder. "I'm not tired. I could stay up with you," she breathed into his ear.

Jane lifted her knee to the mattress and leaned forward to him. She placed her hands on either side of his body and leaned forward farther still. "I need you, Matthew Becker," she said through anticipating lips.

44

Becker strained to hold himself out of reach of her lips. But her warm breath was soothing. He lowered himself down into the bed and surrendered to her request.

Jane followed his movement, climbing onto the bed. She slid her right foot beneath the blanket and straddled him. She began to say something, but he reached up and pulled her down to him, and the rest of her words were lost against his mouth.

The kiss was gentle, prolonging the passion that would follow. Jane knotted her fists in his shirt and pressed her open mouth to his. She dragged his lower lip between her teeth and bit down, drawing it away from his mouth before she released it.

Becker opened his mouth wide as he groaned. Jane licked at his throbbing lip before pressing her mouth to his once more.

His restless hands found the warmth of her bare thighs. He guided his hands to the edge of her silk gown. Grabbing at her thighs, he rocked her body forward, onto him.

Jane stretched out her hands, catching herself before they could collide. She looked into his eyes. "I love you," her voice said, but her eyes said so much more.

Becker held on to the moment. He released his hold of her and reached for her cascading hair. Tucking the strands behind her ears, he revealed her face.

"Jane, I have—"

His words were interrupted by the startling sound of the door intercom. The words that radiated from the speaker were lost in the shattering of the moment.

"It's Lawrence," he repeated. "I need to talk to you."

"Come in, Lawrence," Becker said into the intercom and pressed the lock release.

The front door unlocked. Lawrence stepped through. The entry was hollowed out to house a decontamination holding room. He held his hands out at his sides as the cycle commenced.

Time had executed irreversible damage to the exterior of the home. The stone foundations were eroding. Rotten sidings blended seamlessly into the wet ground. The once-vibrant colors were washed away. But within the walls, where Lawrence stood, the memories of the Becker home lived on.

Every inch of the room was covered in plastic sheeting. Beneath it, the hand-painted floral print on the walls was still visible. The oak shelving housed family photos and medical awards from the late Dr. Becker Senior. Lawrence passed around the room, waiting. The crunch of the plastic beneath his feet did nothing to ease his impatience.

"Make it quick," Becker announced upon his arrival.

"I'd suffocate in here." Lawrence caught himself before leaning on the desolate fireplace mantel.

"We like it here," said Jane dismissively.

"Jane! How are you, my love?" Lawrence turned to look at Jane.

She was beautiful, though not in the common sense of the term. She was the girl you would have met in a small town. The dust kicked up from the fairground would stick to her sweat. She'd look up at you from beneath her baseball cap and smile. The hot day would become a cool summer night, and finally, you would taste the cotton candy on her lips. *What a shame.* Lawrence broke off his gaze.

Jane had felt Lawrence's eyes on her. She had been self-conscious since her bilateral mastectomy surgery. But he didn't stare as others had. How he looked at her then, it wasn't pity. She pulled her robe closed and crossed her arms.

"I'm fine, Lawrence."

Lawrence reached for his pocket watch from within his jacket. *This is all such a waste of time.* Lawrence shut the watch.

"They needed your help, Matt."

Jane spoke ahead of Becker. "You should go," she told Lawrence.

"We have business," Lawrence snapped.

"Jane is right." Becker nodded. "There's nothing that can't wait until morning."

"Is that what you tell yourself when you leave the hospital?" Lawrence knew the question would go unanswered, but he had made his point.

46

CHAPTER 7

Fragile flowers appeared lifeless in the bitter landscape. Blooms peered out from under the trash that littered the planter boxes of Main Street. The small, colored petals would go unnoticed.

The once-quaint downtown was nearly unrecognizable. Over the years of desperation and violence, the city's residents had revolted. The looted buildings were in various states of disrepair. One, in a trio of brick-and-mortar buildings, stood out. Outside the large shop window of that building stood Becker.

His posture was heavy with remorse. He stood there gazing into the ruined building. The interior was recognizable, far less cluttered with debris than the neighboring buildings. Several tables and chairs were set upright; a long counter was intact, with adjacent bar stools.

Becker stepped to one side as he opened the door. He imagined a young boy, eager to play outside, pushing past. He imagined smiling at the boy's mother as she hurried after him.
He took a seat at the counter. "Hello, Mother," Becker greeted her, remembering her in the pink waitress apron she had worn.

Matthew, dear, you're looking well. Oh, but look at your hair. Look how much gray you have now. Don't they sell hair dye in Chicago? she would have said.

"I'm an old man now." Becker brushed over his hair.
You look so much like your father did at your age.

"I'm sorry I haven't visited more since he passed away."
He isn't gone. Not really. His spirit lives on within you.

A shadow passed by the window. Becker turned toward the source. Whatever it was, it was gone. He looked at the diner clock. "I'm going to be late."

Becker removed a towel from a low cabinet and wiped the accumulated dust from the counter. Before he shut the door behind him, he turned back. "There's someone I want you to meet. Her name is Jane."

The soggy morning was cool, but the sky promised sun breaks in the coming day. The silent street lent no ambience to his morning commute. His tired breath hissed through the filter of his mask.

Then he was out of breath. The sight before him was incomprehensible. A swarm of activity. A pair of men were pushing a gurney out the door of the research center. Their bright-yellow hazmat suits were visible to Becker from where he stood, some blocks away.

The Guardian forces took notice of Becker's approach. A trigger-happy trio readied their weapons. A fourth Guardian joined them outside the building.

"Stand down, gentlemen," Marshall ordered. "He works here."

Becker strained for normalcy. "What is all this?" He searched for a familiar face.

"Where is Dr. Ashland?"

"He's right over there." Marshall pointed toward the gurney. "What's left of him, anyway."

Becker followed the gesture. The sheet over the body was drenched with blood.

"My God!" Becker stumbled back.

"God didn't do this," Marshall said.

The CB radio crackled in Marshall's ear. *"Commander Marshall, we've finished our sweep of the perimeter. No sign of them, sir."*

"Acknowledged." Marshall released the CB switch. "What have you unleashed on my city this time, Dr. Becker?"

"I-I don't know what you mean. Where is everyone?"

"Matt! Oh, man, this is a mess." Lawrence stepped through the doorway.

"Lawrence, what's going on here?"

"They're gone. All of them. And something happened to Ash."

"Happened?" Marshall interrupted. "I'll tell you what happened: one of your mutants tore him to pieces. Lord only knows what they did with the innards."

"Mutants?" Becker shot back. "I'll have you know, those were good people in there."

Marshall's voice rang out from the speaker in his mask. "That may have been true, but they're not even people anymore. Whatever unholy things you've done to them, we'll all pay the price."

CHAPTER 8

Lori crouched down, turning back toward Wallace, gesturing that he do the same. Security at the zoo was minimal at night, and Lori was grateful she knew their routines. She watched the Guardian round the corner of the south gate; now they had plenty of time to approach without being seen.

The holding room wouldn't release the inner door without cycling. Lori circled her hands in a swirling motion and nodded to Wallace. *It's going to be very windy.* She hoped he understood. He lowered himself from his towering, cumbersome stance to all fours.

Wallace's fur stood up as the static electricity built in the chamber. Lori could see him becoming uneasy. He shut his eyes tight and placed his paw-like hands over his long, pointed ears.

The cycle ended. Wallace shook himself frantically to settle his fur. Lori found herself admiring his massive physique. *His mutation has made him beautiful.* Looking down at her own hands, she felt no more animal than human. She felt she was neither.

Wallace nuzzled his face into her open hand and whined. Lori hesitated; she didn't want to dehumanize him by petting him. *What do you want?*

———————————————————

Becker followed Lawrence. The two men took shelter behind the thick bushes that circled the clearing.

The pond was located in a central position in the zoo. No matter the path, all eventually led here. And here was as good a place as any to watch her.

50

Lori was knee-deep in the shallows at the edge of the pond. Lawrence couldn't look away from her. She wasn't clothed yet, yet as he opened his eyes to gaze upon her once more, he decided she was not without cover. Her smooth, dark skin dressed her body in lavish ebony shades. He became transfixed with wonder. *Is she a creature now?* Lawrence could not imagine a woman so radiant being categorized that way.

Suddenly, Lori plunged her hand into the water. The splash sent small ripples across the surface of the pond. As she drew back, a thrashing fish was revealed. Lori squeezed her grip around it, sinking in her claws.

Becker pushed back from the bushes and began to stand. His only thought was to be seen, to call out and be known.

"Lori, please, we've come to help," Becker yelled across the pond. His voice was clogged with fear. He realized his fear came from a place of shame, not danger.

Lawrence slowly rose from the cover, recalling the embarrassment of having been caught spying through the window of the ladies' locker room as a child. "Next time, tell me when you're going to do that."

Lori released her kill. As it dropped to the water, she threw her head back. The haunting yowl that came from her gaping mouth was distinctly human, but eerily animal.

Lawrence and Becker began to circle the edge of the water toward Lori. Each step they took closer was guided by the reluctant acceptance that she would flee. Matching their gait, heavy footsteps followed in the nearby underbrush.

"He's stalking us," Lawrence warned.

"No, he's only watching. Has been since we came through the gate," Becker whispered.

As the two men rounded the waterfront, Lori remained still in the water. She watched, turning her head to follow the men's approach. Lori yowled—several short bursts of sound. Again, the noise was a fusion of animal cry and speech.

The response wasn't so much heard as it was felt. The thundering growl shook the men to their core, and its vibrations radiated through them. Wallace was far closer than either of them had thought. The short inhale that followed placed him only a few feet behind.

Lori leapt to the side, gliding across the water like a skipping stone. She retreated, remaining in the shallow water until she was opposite the onlookers, then withdrew from the pond and vanished into the foliage.

Lawrence turned away from the water and scanned the trees. "Do you think he went with her?"

"Yes. Whatever she said, he listened."

"Matt, this is crazy. We're out of our league."

"It was your idea to come here."

"Yeah, but come on, man. You saw what they did to Ash." Lawrence kicked at the dirt.

"So, we leave here empty-handed?" Becker hunched over to look Lawrence in the eye.

"The big cats exhibit is past the elephants. It's, it's this way. Good a place as any to look for them." Lawrence sighed.

The lion paid them no mind as they circled its enclosure. His large head and shaggy mane rested on outstretched legs. The fur was waning and dull. Becker paused a moment to observe as the lioness emerged from the shelter. The mood in the enclosure shifted. The lion was suddenly very aware of the onlookers. He rose to a prominent stance by his queen. *He would die for her.* Becker pictured Jane in his mind.

"You coming?" Lawrence looked back at Becker.

The path ended at a stairwell, where a sign read "Observation Deck." The lynx enclosure was cut into the rising ground, and the adjacent building blocked the view.

Becker nodded to the steps. "We can get a good look from up there."

"I don't know, Matt. Seems odd to me that they'd break into a prison. You saw the other animals back there—they want to be set free."

"Lori and Wallace aren't animals. They're just afraid. The changes in their bodies are foreign."

"You're not saying they're human, are you?"

"What does it mean to be human?" Becker asked. It was a question he himself could not answer.

The deck was open on one side for viewing. The rest was enclosed with walls and a continuous awning. Several display stands cluttered the floor. Each was dedicated to a specific purpose: the reconstruction of the zoo, the dome, the decontamination chamber, and a memorial for all the men and women who'd given their lives to keep *'the dream of a better tomorrow alive.'*

Becker thought of his father's plaque: *The people's doctor.* The inscription was simple. His father served the people of Franklin City. All people. No matter their race, religion, or orientation. That philosophy had to continue now. No matter how *they* were labeled.

Lawrence turned and leaned against the railing of the terrace. "Matthew," he said, transfixed. "She's behind you."

Becker turned slowly, following Lawrence's gaze. Lori stepped out from behind a display, revealing herself fully. Lawrence backed toward the stairs, keeping his focus on her.

"Lori, we've come to help you." Becker approached with his hands open at his sides.

She kept her eyes on him as she lowered herself to the ground until her clawed fingers scratched the floor. Lori crawled backward. She moved with such fluidity and grace that Becker watched in awe. Then he stepped forward to follow.

"Watch out!" Lawrence yelled from the top of the stairs.

A large display came crashing down at Becker's feet. Then the only sound was breathing. Wallace's nostrils flared with each breath.

His silhouette was that of a man. He stood tall above the wrecked display. His dark skin was split open like tree bark. He curled his lips to expose his canine teeth and released a thunderous growl.

"Wallace. Wallace, are you in there?" Becker stumbled back.

"No!" Wallace barked.

He leapt forward, striking Becker in his midsection. The heavy blow knocked the wind out of him. Becker felt the railing at his back, then watched everything fade into the distance as he fell to the ground below.

Becker lay in shock in the lynx enclosure. As he felt himself losing consciousness, he made a mental diagnosis of his injuries: *bimalleolar fracture, tibia shaft fracture, vertebral compression fracture . . .*

CHAPTER 9

Rhian had been a fidgety child, never still outside her slumber. She wore pencils dull and pens dry as her teachers droned on about everything—while she felt they said nothing. She would draw in the margins of her books, dreaming of her next return to the stage. Illustrations of ballet slippers with interwoven laces. A gown, elegant and free-flowing. A *mask* to put on and change who she was. Where she was.

Rhian twirled on her forefoot, paused, and raised herself to the tip of her toes. She posed her arms high above her head in a pyramid, then lowered them gracefully to her sides. A gentle leap to one side. She twirled once more before she saw him.

Drake was peering through the gaping hole in the wall from the neighboring room. He hadn't meant to be silent for so long.

"Veronica is awake. We should all talk," Drake said, turning away.

Rhian relaxed her stance and sighed.

Veronica looked much better today, Rhian thought as she approached her. She was sitting on a metal desk chair, gazing out into the morning mist. She drew a porcelain mug to her lips and sipped the mucky rainwater.

Rhian cringed. "Maybe I could go for a supplies run. I don't think you should be drinking that."

"That's impossible. We can't leave," Drake said, scratching his arm.

"'Why, sometimes I've believed as many as six impossible things before breakfast,'" Rhian recited.

"Look around. Do you see any breakfast?" Drake snapped.

"Here, we must run as fast as we can, just to stay in place. And if you wish to go anywhere, you must run twice as fast as that," Rhian exclaimed.

"She's quoting *Alice in Wonderland*, honey," Veronica chimed in.

"And how much farther down the *rabbit hole* could we possibly go?" Drake said.

"I'll tell you one thing: I need to shave if I'm going out there." Rhian looked down at her bare legs.

"You can borrow whatever you need from Lucy's room. I don't think she's coming back." Veronica stood from the chair. "I'll show you to her room."

"Mrs. Casper and . . . I don't believe I've had the pleasure, Ms. . . . ?" Miles, the brothel-keeper, stood in the doorway to Veronica's room.

"Feist," Rhian answered.

"Feist, is it? And here I thought Veronica was the *feisty* one." Miles chuckled.

"What do you want, Miles?" Veronica sneered.

"Well, it seems to be all about what *you* want these days. I've given you back your old job, and I understand you've been closed for business? And now I find you with this young thing. Where are you two off to, then, huh?" Miles blocked the exit with his arm.

"We were going to borrow some things from Lucy."

"Ah, Lucy. I see. What a shame she left. You're taking her place, then, I take it?" Miles looked at Rhian with a hungry smile.

"I work at the theater. I'm an actress," Rhian said, fumbling for words.

"Well." Miles puffed up his chest. "There's no better job for an *actress* than here at The Red Tent. Why, I put a roof over your head and see that you never go hungry. All I ask is that you show our guests the same hospitality."

"I'm late for a very important date!" Rhian ducked under his arm to reach the hall.

"Goodbye, *Rabbit*." Veronica laughed.

Miles turned to watch Rhian walk away. "Rabbit, huh? That explains the fuzzy legs."

"I explained our *treatment* when we got here." Veronica looked back at Miles.

"Ha! And it's a good thing you did. I would have thought the circus was in town."

Veronica looked down at her hands. She thought she could be the main attraction at the circus freak show. *Head of a beautiful girl. Body of an ugly snake.* She had seen the banner before, but she never wanted to look inside. Now she only had to look in the mirror.

"We didn't take it all that well at first, either, if that's any consolation."

"Listen, Veronica, work with the lights off for all I care, but you will work. I've lost too many girls for you to not be working."

"I understand." Veronica closed the door.

"You can hear the baby's heartbeat now." Dr. Kranes held the fetal Doppler to Veronica's swollen belly.

"How far along is she, Doc?" Rhian asked, pulling a piece of gum from her open pack.

"She seems to be in her second trimester, so that would be at least thirteen weeks.

"Although, with these *changes* to your body, Veronica, I can't be sure." Kranes felt the Doppler glide across her scale-like skin.

Rhian blew a big pink bubble. *Pop.* "What, she's going to, like, lay an egg or something?"

"Rabbit!" Veronica cringed. "Did you find any prenatals while you were out?"

"Yeah, snake mama." Rhian reached for her backpack.

"Is she a mutant too?" Kranes asked in a hushed voice.

"Our little *rabbit* didn't mutate like Drake and I, but yes, she's one of us. Seems her white fuzz is about the extent of it. Pretty thing goes through razors, though, I can tell you."

"If she had the Varivax vaccine as a child, her skin wouldn't be as damaged by the virus. Maybe that means there would be less mutation." Kranes watched Rhian finish packing up her bag to leave.

"You seem to know an awful lot about it. Did you work at the research center before Dr. Becker?"

56

Dr. Becker? His being there came as a surprise. It had been years since Kranes had been under his care, but still, he remembered Becker being a more *conventional* doctor.

"No, I've just met someone who had the vaccine. They do much better with treatment than . . . " Kranes looked at Veronica. Her eyes were growing soft.

"I'm sorry. You and your baby seem to be in good health. There's really nothing to worry about." The doctor wiped the gel from Veronica's stomach.

"How is she?" Drake asked, entering the apartment.

"Where have you been?" Veronica pulled her shirt down.

"Miles told me to fix a leak in the roof."

"And that was more important than being here?"

"Miranda's ceiling was swollen with water. She threatened to leave like the others if it didn't get fixed," Drake shouted from the kitchen back to the living room.

"Excuse me." Kranes flinched as he stepped between the arguing couple. "How many women did you say have left?"

"I didn't say. But now that you mention it, there've been quite a few." Drake opened an old bag of jerky and inhaled the scent before pulling a piece out. "Why do ask?"

"My employer has tasked me with keeping some young ladies in good health. Do you know where the ones who leave end up?"

"Well, no. And I thought Miles was your boss?" Veronica sat up from the couch.

"The Boss *uses* them. I should have realized it. *Oh, God.* How could I have missed it?"

"What are you babbling about?" Drake chewed on the dry meat.

Kranes gasped, his heart pounding. "I must have done a dozen surgeries by now. I try not to look at their faces. They're all dead because of me!" Kranes dropped his medical bag and began to sob.

"Hold on. Were they infected?" Veronica grabbed Kranes' shoulder to turn him toward her.

"No! Don't you see, I used their healthy organs to save her men."

Drake approached the doctor. "Where can we find this *boss* of yours?" he demanded, as he held a kitchen knife to the doctor's throat.

"The warehouse. It's the only one with power. I warn you, though, she has an army of men."

"It seems she has you to thank for that," Veronica concluded.

"You're taking up residency here at The Red Tent from now on," Drake demanded of Kranes.

"What are you thinking, Drake?" Veronica asked.

"I have a plan."

CHAPTER 10

The room was as thick in dust as it was dark. The air was stale and would have been motionless if not for the cracked panes of glass letting in warm air. Bothered by the smell, a man secured his handkerchief around his lower face. Aiming the narrow beam from his flashlight, he uncovered the obstacles in the darkness. Large pieces of equipment were strategically placed; as many to be moved as there were men to move them. The foreman directed the workforce of distressed men.

The men strained to see in the dim lights of their headlamps. What lay ahead, as they unfastened the heavy equipment from the warehouse floor, was fleeing rats, shards of metal debris, and grueling hours of work. They felt for each anchor bolt, finding them with outstretched fingers. Attaching crude wrenches to each of the rusty nuts, they pried with all their strength, as if to remove the symbolic restraints that kept them there.

Crooked backs and torn muscles throbbed from the unremitting efforts to maintain sufficient progress. Beyond the limits of any one of them, the men worked together to remove the equipment. Even the protruding bolts were cut off, the floor hand-filed smooth.

At last, they came to the final obstacle. The printing press.

The door to the building swung open, but the exhausted men lay still. The foreman had returned to the building site after his brief, but ultimately satisfactory, absence.

"She said our debt has been cleared!" Thomas announced. He noticed the press.

"Wait, what the hell is that still doing here?"

"It's welded to supports in the concrete. There's no way to move it," said one of the men.

"Take it down piece by piece if you have to!" As the men got to their feet, the nearly dead lights they carried provided little help to their awareness. A vibrant burst of match light suddenly sparked in the warehouse.

"Maybe you didn't hear the man," The Boss said, after lighting her cigarette.

Each of the men had his own story of how he'd arrived here, but all the stories had the same horrific points. They became infected, in need of organ transplant. The Boss promised to extend their lives, but at a cost.

Joe drew his gun and forced Thomas to his knees.

"I'm sorry, Boss. They told me it would be done." Thomas cringed, raising his hands in a meager defense.

The Boss nodded to Joe. Blood splattered her white dress as Joe pulled the trigger. The gaping head wound was visible to all in the flash of the gunshot; it left little to the imagination for the remaining men. Fall short of paying your debt and you would pay the ultimate price.

"Leave the machine, gentlemen. I may have a use for it yet," The Boss called, heading toward her office.

"Joe," The Boss said as she turned to face him, "bring the car around. I want to go to the park."

———————————————

The rusty chain of the swing squealed in resistance to the motion. The Boss slowed to a stop, her legs limp beneath the seat. She looked at Joe, who had been continually surveying the park. Any onlookers would take notice of the motion inside the dome.

Joe snarled at the idea of being spotted. "We should get going soon."

The Boss reached down and dug her feet into the gravel beneath the swing. The cold rocks tickled her bare feet. "You've always been here for me," she said, not looking up from her feet.

Joe bent down and scooped up her shoes. "That's my job," he said, holding the shoes out to her. "Here, put these on."

60

The Boss slid off the seat and stepped over to Joe. She took the shoes from him and continued past. "I didn't know that it was your job back then. I just remember you always being there." Her voice showed her emotions rising.

Joe removed his handkerchief from his jacket and approached.

"I know, Boss. I was happy to do it." Joe handed over the cloth.

The Boss wiped beneath her eyes to gather her tears. She sniffed. "Are you happy now?" She bit hard on her lower lip to keep from bursting out, but it only made her tears fall faster.

Retreating from her memories, she reached down to her garter and slid out her cigarette case. "Got a light?" she asked.

Joe patted his jacket and looked around. He reached into his inner pocket and pulled out a book of matches. The strike of the match as Joe leaned in to light her cigarette revealed her face. He paused as she took in the first drag. The night had revealed a second face, one behind the mask of The Boss.

"Wait, there's someone out there," Joe exclaimed, looking past her, to the street beyond.

The Boss turned quickly to look. She stumbled a few steps forward, trying to bend down and slip on her shoes. "Who else would be out here?" she asked, peering through the night air.

Joe zeroed in on the potential prey. "Rhian Feist." He watched the figure dart across the street, toward the park. "I'd recognize her anywhere."

"Who?"

"She's an actress at the theater. At least, she was. I could have sworn she was infected."

"She doesn't look infected to me, Joe. Go get the car."

"But I sent her flowers, your flowers."

"You what?" The Boss asked, outraged.

"I thought if we were both infected—"

"What, that I would save her life and you two could be together? Go get the car, Joe!"

Rhian stopped as she noticed the two figures inside the dome. Her vision was better than it had ever been, especially at night. She looked at The Boss only briefly; she was more struck by Joe's appearance. She made a move to retreat from the park's entrance.

The chase began.

CHAPTER 11

The hospital was exactly like she had expected. The walls had once been painted—a pale yellow. Jane could tell by the flakes on the floor. The framed photographs that still hung on the walls were dull in the windowless corridor. The floor was uneven with broken tiles; she had a hard time imagining a stretcher not getting stuck. The stagnant air was laced with mold and made the space feel cave-like. Had it not been for the naked fluorescent tubes flickering above, the hallway would have seemed dead.

The hum of the lights nagged at her ears like a buzzing fly. Jane jerked her head to one side and waved the relentless buzz from her mind. A single exhale of relief followed—before the dull roar became overpowering once more.

Jane squeezed her eyes shut. A steady stream of tears poured from them. Her mouth opened in a silent scream. She choked on the void of air in her throat. Her body shivered as she took in a sliver of air through chattering teeth.

Comfort had been a pointless pursuit; it was impossible to settle in the chair. Jane let her trembling hands rest in her lap and lowered her throbbing head. At last, somewhere between dreaming and drowning, she found a moment's rest at the hospital.

"Jane?" Lawrence repeated, attempting to wake her. "You can see him now."

Jane pulled away from her nightmare and awoke to see Lawrence seated next to her.

"He's awake," Lawrence continued. He placed an arm around her shoulders and brought her into his chest. He swallowed down his emotions as his eyes welled up.

"I could really use your help. Doctors are the worst patients." Lawrence laughed, pushing through his miserable emotion.

"Do you really think he'll walk again?" Jane asked, pulling back to look at his flooded eyes.

"That's up to Matt now. I've done everything I can," Lawrence said, rubbing his face with the sleeve of his white jacket.

Lawrence led Jane down another hallway. They each had about as much personality as the interstate, she thought. They stopped outside one of the many identical doorways.

"Jane." Lawrence held her back from the door. "You understand why I had to do this?"

"I've watched him lie there for months. Some days I felt invisible. Yes, Lawrence, we need him to come back. I need to see him smile again."

Opening the door revealed an all-too-familiar motif of exposed concrete and chipped paint. Jane looked at the small window. In an attempt to keep anyone from opening it, plexiglass was screwed to the frame. She imagined someone so desperate to die that they would open it. She lowered her eyes at the thought.

The bed sat low to the ground. Jane avoided looking right at it. The frame was rusted, and she could see the edge of the mattress was worn thin. She turned her head away and looked at Lawrence. Finally, she looked at Becker, lying naked, facedown on the bed.

"I used a biomaterial base around the protrusions. This will act as a dermal layer, so the epidermal layer can graft," Lawrence began.

Jane's mind refused to take in the sight all at once. She focused instead on the bolts sticking out from his leg on either side of the knee. The soft tissue had been cut in a two-inch circle around the bolt.

"Graft?" she asked in a hollow voice.

"His skin will cover up to the flange around the bolt." Lawrence pointed.

"I didn't realize there would be so many—" Jane gasped. Her eyes shifted to his elbow, where another pair of bolts neighbored the joint.

64

"The extent of his spinal injuries would never have allowed full function of his limbs. This way, we have a permanent anchor point for the exoskeleton." Lawrence nodded to the open case on the end table.

Jane felt the color in her face drain and her stomach turn over. She took in the horrific spectacle down his back. Each exposed vertebrae of his spine was joined with a metal jacket. Connecting each plate to the next were micro struts and tension coil springs.

Jane's composure was ripped away. Her eyes darted about the room, in search of a waste basket to catch her vomit. She looked to the one place she hadn't before: beneath the table, where a mirror lay on the floor. She caught Becker's reflection. His face rested in an opening in the bed. Jane broke into a smirk of playful disgust, masking her true nausea roiling in her stomach.

With a wrinkled nose, Jane took a step back from the bed. "What can I do to help?" she asked, glancing back at Lawrence.

"Help me get him dressed, and then I'll show you how everything fits."

"Matt?" Jane placed her hand on his shoulder. "Is that okay with you?"

Becker flinched at her touch.

"Now, Jane, the incisions have all been cauterized, so you don't have to worry about bleeding. That being said, you'll need to be careful not to stress the skin." Lawrence took hold of Becker's foot and bent his leg back at the knee. He pointed to the incisions around the bolts of the joint. "Until his skin has grafted to the biomaterial base, there's a risk of breaking the connection loose here, you see?"

Becker stirred in the bed. He began to raise his elbows and placed his palms on the mattress. He strained to push off the bed, lifting his face from the porthole in the mattress. "I've had enough."

Lawrence and Jane stepped to either side of him. They grabbed hold of his shoulders and helped him push himself onto his hands and knees. Resisting any further help, Becker struggled into a seated position on the edge of the bed. Realizing he didn't have the strength to continue alone, he said, "Let's get this over with."

Jane brought his underwear and slacks as high up his legs as she could before hitting the mattress. She carefully slid one arm into the sleeve of his shirt, then the other. As she finished buttoning the shirt, she looked into Matt's eyes. "I love you."

Becker's chest rose as he took in a deep breath. Jane could hear the stress of the springs in his spinal support network. A twinge of pain froze his face.

He released the air slowly out of his nose and then pushed out a single word in response: "Don't."

Jane turned toward Lawrence. She fluttered her eyes to try to keep tears from forming. "Will you help me stand him up?" she asked.

Becker pushed off the bed and staggered on weak legs, trying to find his balance. "Stop talking about me like I'm not right here." He made several attempts to grab the band of his underwear, but his fingers were limp.

"Please, let me help you." Jane extended her arms out in offering. Becker nodded. He looked away as she bent down to finish dressing him.

"Are you going to let us finish here?" Lawrence asked, reaching for the case on the table. He removed an entanglement of cables and gears, held it at arm's length, and stepped around Becker to begin hooking him up. Jane watched carefully, already understanding the basic parts.

"You begin by placing the two straps over the shoulders. Then you fasten each geared tension coil at the joints." Each of the fastening bolts stuck through the specially tailored garb.

"There's plenty of slack in the cables from the fixed point of each bolt to here." Lawrence pointed to the center of Becker's back.

Jane nodded. "But how will all of this help him walk?"

Lawrence threw her an annoyed glance as he finished threading the tension coils on either side of the knee. "These are spring-loaded. The tension will help keep the joint from collapsing. After he steps through, the coil unwinds and helps straighten his leg again."

Becker raised his fists up to his chest, and then allowed the coils to pull his arms back to his sides. "What if I don't have the strength?"

Lawrence went back to the case. He removed a disc the size of a Frisbee. "Each time you move any of the four joints, the cogs of the interlocking gears pull the cables. Once there is enough tension on the cable, it will automatically pop loose and spin this central flywheel."

Lawrence stepped over to Becker's back and affixed the wheel. "This allows for a short-term storage of energy. As long as it's spinning, you can channel the movement back through the cables to any pair of joints by using this." Lawrence lifted a small device hanging at Becker's side. "You'll want to hold on to this at all times. You see here, there are two levers. One for your legs, and one for your arms."

Lawrence placed the control box in Becker's hand. He then traced the cable that ran from the box to the wheel. "Everything seems to be in order. Let's see how you do."

Jane stood in front of Becker and reached for his hands. "You have to try."

Becker lifted both hands to his chest in repetitions. By his tenth set, they could hear the tension release and spin the flywheel.

"Good. Now, pull the first lever back slightly," Lawrence instructed.

Becker glared, but he did as he was told. Both of his arms lifted again, but this time without his own force. When they reached his chest, the tension released, and the coil pulled them back to straight.

"You've turned me into a windup toy," Becker huffed.

Jane wasn't sure if it was her imagination, but she could have sworn she saw a smile, *no matter how slight*, forming on Becker's mouth.

"Good to see you haven't lost your sense of humor, Matt." Lawrence laughed. "Now, let's see how you can get around."

Becker pressed on, trying to avoid the assistance of the wheel. Jane watched from a few steps ahead in the hall. She had tried to hold his arm, but he refused it. "You're doing great, Matthew," she encouraged.

Becker looked up from his feet to Jane, then ahead to the exit of the hospital. "I want to get out of here," he declared.

Jane followed Becker's gaze to the exit. She saw three masks paired with heavy rain jackets on a series of hooks just inside the door. "Well, I guess we could get some fresh air." She laughed.

She helped Becker secure his mask, then put hers on. They stepped into the holding room and waited for the system to cycle and the exterior doors to open.

The parking lot was a demolition derby. Several cars had been burned out, leaving scorched metal frames and melted tires. The entrance and exits were clogged with crunched vehicles, forever intertwined with one another where they were left. Several semis blocked the emergency entrance of the hospital, their trailers loaded with decomposed bodies.

There was an all-but-forgotten story outside the hospital. The infected had died in waves. The surviving family members followed close behind. They paid the ultimate price for love; the virus spared no one.

Becker flinched at the surge of memories. He saw himself covering the deceased with a white sheet. One after another. Dozens. Hundreds. Many had been loaded into tractor-trailers and hauled away. Still, he carried the weight of each death. "We never had a chance." He sighed.

Jane reached for his hand. "You can't give up now."

Becker interlocked his fingers with hers and swallowed down his emotions. "I don't know if I'm strong enough to take all the pain. How can I help them when it takes everything I have to move? It all hurts, Jane. My body. My mind. Every time I close my eyes, I see death. I welcome it."

Jane took in the words. Squeezing his hand tight, she tilted her head toward his shoulder. Jane tried to escape the darkness of his words with her own. Every word fell short of a response, until she pleaded, "Let me take care of you."

The couple continued walking in silence for some time. Becker had long passed fatigue, but he refused to rely on the flywheel. They rounded the corner and paused across from the theater. Becker was quick to recognize Rhian out front. The sight of her was striking. He was in awe of her physical health. Yet, he soon became aware of the fear on her face. Her expression cried out for help.

Becker stumbled off the curb to approach her. He felt Jane pull him back and then saw the blur of the passing vehicle.

Joe swung open the driver's-side door as the tires screeched to a halt. He was first to reach Rhian, with Babu closing the distance behind.

"I told you to wait in the car, dummy. I got this," Joe barked.

The passenger-side rear door opened slowly. The Boss set her feet on the ground. She rose from the car and pulled her dress down to cover her legs. She grabbed Becker's interest.

Her beauty could not be denied, even amongst the chaos. The subtle pout of her full lips, smeared with gleaming gloss, demanded attention. But her eyes, her eyes showed her true self. They were deep pools of sadness surrounded by stormy skies of blue-gray. Deeper still, he was drawn into her. There, he saw the lightning spark in a place where darkness was desire. Far more than a gleam in her eye, the spark had shown him that she had a place among the storm.

Babu had grabbed Rhian, and he held her to face Joe. She kicked and thrashed, desperate to flee. Then Rhian screamed for help. Everyone in the theater would have heard it. She jerked back to see the entrance. The door remained closed. Motionless. It was as if it were vacant. *What is wrong with you people?*

Becker tried to step forward but found only agony; his strength had long left him. He reached for the control box for his suit and pressed the lever. His strained legs pushed forward.

He couldn't hear Jane yelling to him. At this moment, all he could hear was the flywheel disc on his back. Becker pushed the lever to full release. He felt the pavement beneath him twist away. He stumbled through each step, barely finding the ground before it was gone again. Then the movement stopped. He stopped.

Becker had charged into Babu, who was now sprawled out on the ground. Back to the entrance of the theater, Becker slid down the door to sit on the step. He grabbed his throbbing shoulder. *Anterior dislocation. Clavicle fracture.* He squinted in pain.

He saw Joe pulling Rhian to the car. He clutched a fistful of her hair as he screamed at her.

The Boss was approaching Becker. He tilted his head to see Jane gaining on her. Jane grabbed her wrist and yanked her so they were eye-to-eye.

"Back off, bitch!" Jane yelled.

With a heavy backhand, Jane slapped The Boss with everything she had.

Babu groaned as he sat up. He shook his head as clear as it would come. With little effort, he tossed Jane to Becker's side. She cried out in pain as she struck the door.

"Sorry, lady," Babu said to Jane.

"Don't apologize!" The Boss shrieked, rubbing her cheek.

The driver's-side door swung open, and Rhian reached out, screaming.

"You wanna help me here?" Joe yelled, grasping at Rhian.

The Boss looked back at Babu and then nodded to Joe. "We got what we came for, boys. Let's go."

CHAPTER 12

The Boss removed the baggie of corn syrup from the freezer and held it to her swollen face. The lights in the room flickered as the freezer began to cycle. She bent down to unplug it from the extension cord. "Not a word, Joe, not one word."

Joe stood by the door of the office, keeping his eyes on the floor. Three heavy-fisted knocks struck the door. Joe took out his pistol and placed his other hand on the knob. "Who is it?"

"Uhhh . . ." Babu blanked. Joe could hear two other voices through the door. Babu repeated their introductions. "Miles Drake."

"What?" Joe snapped.

Babu listened again. "Oh, Miles *and* Drake."

"We've come to talk to your boss," Miles shouted.

The Boss looked at Joe for an explanation. He shook his head.

Drake cut through the tension of waiting, calling from outside, "I believe you know Dr. Kranes. He thought it was time we all met."

"Where is Kranes now?" The Boss paused from lighting her cigarette.

Joe shrugged. "Haven't seen him for a few days, Boss."

"Ouch!" The Boss shook the match out as it burned down to her finger. "Let them in."

"Please allow me to introduce The Red Tent's very own cannibal of miscreants, The Dragon," Miles announced as he entered.

The Boss applauded sarcastically. "Well, that was theatrical." She stood from her desk. "*Cannibal of miscreants*, does that mean you're going to eat me?" The Boss stepped over to Drake.

Miles felt the sweat build on his brow in the heat of his mask. He realized he was the only person in the room wearing one. He glanced at Drake to find him mesmerized by the femme fatale.

"We came to tell you that we're done supplying you with spare parts!" Miles barked.

"Sorry? It's hard to hear you with that thing on your face." The Boss motioned with disgust. "Why don't you take it off?"

"What? No, I can't. Listen, we got off on the wrong foot here. Drake! Drake, you said you would help me! Wha-what's going on?" Miles realized that his mask was not the only reason he stood out as different. They were *all* looking down at him.

"Drake? I thought you said his name was Dragon." The Boss shifted her gaze from Miles back to Drake.

Babu pulled Miles's arms behind him. He squirmed like a beached eel but grew tired quickly, his breathing becoming labored. Babu lowered him to his knees. Joe approached Miles, holding out a bottle to him.

"Do you know what this is? I bet you can't guess." Joe unscrewed the cap and sniffed at the contents. "You're not at a disadvantage with your mask. It's odorless, colorless, and hell, even tasteless." Joe poured the contents of the bottle over Miles's head and mask. He tried to shake off as much of the liquid as he could.

"Ahem," The Boss interrupted, an unlit cigarette on her lips.

"See, when The Boss asks for something, I listen." Joe pulled a matchbook from his jacket and produced a light. He turned back to Miles. "But you're not a boss." Joe dropped the match.

Babu release his hold as Miles was set ablaze. His hair singed down to his scalp within an instant. The rubber of his mask was melting to his face. He pulled on it frantically, desperate to remove it. The filter cartridge collapsed and cut off the airflow. His screams grew faint. Miles spent the last moments of his life suffocating and burning.

"As you can see, I don't need a *dragon* to set my fires." The Boss perched herself on the corner of her desk.

"He wanted to cut off your supply. I can tell you where to find them."

"Oh, Dragon, I know where they came from. I also know where you came from. You're nothing more than a science experiment. Komodo dragon DNA, really? And now you think you're special. Don't make me laugh." The Boss drew on her cigarette as she taunted him.

"You said your doctor is missing, right?" said Drake. "What if I can help you find a replacement?"

"And who might that be?" The Boss stubbed out her cigarette on the desktop.

"Dr. Becker. He's the one who did this to us. And he's a surgeon. Just what you need, right?"

"*Us*, you say? You mean the other animals, Rabbit and Viper?" She took pleasure in seeing his shocked reaction to the given names. "We have that frisky furball already. She's a talker, that one. Now, your snake woman—I can't wait to meet *her*."

"You leave Veronica out of this!"

"Not so loud." Babu groaned. The Boss winked at Babu in gratitude.

"I've actually been thinking it's time I had a talk with Dr. Becker. We have some unfinished business. Why don't you bring your Viper back here, and I'll set up the reunion, okay?"

The Boss circled her desk and lowered herself onto the seat. "Oh, and Dragon? You may leave here with your life, but don't forget who owns it. You work for me now."

Drake responded with a single nod of acceptance.

CHAPTER 13

Jane and Lawrence carefully lowered Becker down to lie on his dining table.

"Thank you for coming, Lawrence. It seems pretty bad," Jane said.

Becker grimaced in pain. His shoulder had been displaced for many hours. Lawrence stood beside him and took hold of his right hand. He bent the arm at the elbow and brought Becker's hand up over his head. He continued to push until Becker's fingertips touched the opposite shoulder.

"There we go." Lawrence heaved. The crunching shift of the dislocation came to fruition.

"I guess I should learn how to do that if you're going to keep running around town beating up bad guys," Jane teased.

"Running?" Lawrence raised an eyebrow.

"It was the suit. Jane and I had been walking." Becker sat up on the table. "And I used all the stored energy at once." He rubbed his sore shoulder.

"One second he was right in front of me, the next he was across the street." Jane snapped her fingers. "Just like that."

"Faster than a speeding bullet, eh?" Lawrence chuckled.

"Like a *bullet*—yes, exactly!" Jane joined in with the giggles.

"I'm glad you find this so amusing, but I'm not a superhero."

"You *are* a hero to Franklin City," Lawrence said.

Jane smiled. "I've always said so."

"They will call me *Bullet*," Becker croaked, attempting an old-movie-style vigilante voice.

Jane and Lawrence closed in around him, helping him to stand as they all shared a laugh.

"I should get going." Lawrence broke away. "Marshall has assembled a team to hunt down Wallace and Lori since they fled the zoo."

"I saw Rhian," Becker mumbled. "She didn't look anything like the others. In fact, she didn't seem to have mutated at all."

"How is that possible?"

Jane entered the conversation. "She had the chickenpox vaccine, right? Like that little girl, Samantha."

"Is that right?" Lawrence looked at Becker.

Becker froze.

"Matt?" Lawrence nudged him.

"Matthew!" Jane took hold of him as he began to slump over.

The intercom buzzer sounded. Lawrence jerked his head toward the sound, then turned back to Jane. "Just go. I have him." Jane stumbled as she helped Becker to reach a dining chair.

Lawrence looked at the monitor in the kitchen. The view was blocked by a piece of paper. Large, black, printed text dominated the pale sheet.

You have not been forgotten. We offer ORGAN TRANSPLANTS. Your future begins here. Old Town Industrial District.

Joe turned the page over and held it back up to the camera. A handwritten note was shown. *Dr. Becker, your patients need you. — Samantha "The Boss" Angeline.*

Lawrence remained at the monitor after the messenger had left. He could hear the couple approaching down the hall. Jane was supporting Becker. Their words fell short of breaking Lawrence's daze.

"Can you give us a hand?" Jane yelled, trying again.

Lawrence smacked his hand on the wall. "She wants Becker!"

"Who does? Who was at the door?" Jane was straining under Becker's weight.

Lawrence saw her bewilderment and described the notice and the letter.

Becker straightened his back and found his balance. "The woman tonight was Samantha. They abducted Rhian, and she must already have the others. That's what she meant by my *patients*."

Lawrence looked at Becker. "She's using them as leverage, Matt. She wants you back in surgery."

"'I will respect the hard-won scientific gains of those physicians in whose steps I walk.'" Becker leaned on the wall and continued reciting. "'And gladly share such knowledge as is mine with those who are to follow.'"

"I remember the oath, but you can't *gladly share* a damn thing if you're dead," Lawrence argued.

Jane stood by Becker on the wall. "Please don't do this."

"I won't go." Becker clenched his fists. *Bullet will.*

CHAPTER 14

The morning sky looked like an unfinished painting. Golden sunlight burst from the dawn on one side, with a seamless smear of white clouds on the other. The approaching storm would overtake the sun soon.

Lawrence released his foot from the accelerator. The old truck motor sputtered and died. He leaned over and, with a circular motion, whipped away the fog of the passenger window. With his sight clear, he became all the more muddled. He saw the shop window. Through it, a caged fox was visible. He wouldn't have stopped or even noticed the animal as he passed by if not for the most uncommon of sights — the neon sign above the door. *Open*. Lawrence spent a moment staring at the glow from the sign. The truck window was pelted by rain as the moment grew longer. Soon, the neon glow was spread across a mosaic of droplets. Lawrence slid off the truck seat to the flooded ground. He began his slow walk to The Guardian headquarters.

Lawrence leaned against the wall beside the office door. He had been waiting long enough to hear Marshall reprimand the men inside. Donny and Travis offered few words in response. That was why Lawrence had picked them. *Simple boys*. They'd be dead by now, had they not enlisted. The door opened. The pair stepped out, and each man paused to salute. Lawrence nodded in response. He'd had contracts with the military for years, long before all of this. He hadn't enlisted then, and he wouldn't now.

Lawrence stepped into the office and took a seat at the desk. "Samantha took over her father's business."

"Samantha?" Marshall questioned.

"Yes, Samantha *Angeline*," Lawrence said, pointing to his own right eye.

"I'll issue a Guardian order at once!"

"Maybe you should sit this one out," Lawrence put forward. "Unplug for a while."

"You want me to turn the other cheek? Not this time."

Lawrence left his meeting with Marshall. He opened the doors before him, and his eyes fluttered as they adjusted to the light coming in. The sun, which was now sliding down the far corner of the sky, pierced the clouds. Over the years they had not been able to see the sun often due to the clouds and the constant rain, but now the burning mass occasionally peeked out. Little signs like these brought the idea of hope, that what they had done to the planet was reversible.

He walked out onto the cracked pavement, squatted, and studied the consistency of the soil. Even with the gloves, he could see that it was dry and gritty. When he got up, he could feel a dull ache traveling down his right leg as he did so—*old age*, he thought.

The city before him lay desolated. Silence drifted through the littered streets as he saw the wind picking up, blowing dirt and whatever garbage that was lodged between vehicles and the surrounding buildings in the area. An empty bag of chips landed on his mask, obstructing his vision briefly before he quickly removed it, clearly frustrated. Even now, the terrible habits of the previous civilization still lingered, and it probably would be here for a long time.

As he walked past the towering buildings, Lawrence half expected to see the pigeons hovering over the edge of the building to release themselves on the unsuspecting bystanders casually walking beneath them. But the bystanders were nowhere to be found; not for a while now.

He observed what was within his line of sight. The parts of the road and among the trees, looking for any movement. He had been on guard since seeing what Wallace and Lori had become.

Once he stepped off the uneven pavement and made it onto the road, the pain in his leg intensified. He carried a gun in his belt with the safety off. There were fifteen rounds he could get out of it before he needed to reload it again. He was hoping it wouldn't come to that since he had no extra ammo.

Lawrence journeyed down the road. He passed the abandoned cars that were scattered around the dismal city. They all stood there, some with doors left wide open like rusted ghosts waiting for their owners to return. Time was slowly devouring the remains of one of man's greatest inventions.

It wasn't long before the sun hid behind the clouds again and a loud boom rolled across the gray skies. He was only a few blocks out from where the truck was parked, but Lawrence knew he wouldn't make it in time. Another crash of thunder ripped through the sky, and this time a heavy downpour followed. He ran the rest of the way, feeling his boots sinking into the exposed mud on the ground, and he groaned, knowing how difficult it was going to be to remove it. Lawrence was never a fan of the rain; in fact, he hated it. He hated the way it felt on his skin, how it made the world look cold and depressing.

He could spot the old truck parked along the sidewalk where it had died. Lawrence pulled the door open, and water from the oncoming shower drenched the interior. He retrieved the key and stuck it into the ignition. As Lawrence turned the key, he waited for the engine to turn. *Please, please, please*, he thought as he laid his head on the wheel.

He could hear the starter trying to turn the engine over but stopping halfway. If it didn't start soon, he would have to travel to Becker's by foot, and given the rain, the idea was not very appealing. He tried once more and the motor roared to life. Lawrence put the truck in gear, smiling for the first time in a while, and turned down the street.

CHAPTER 15

Rhian was on her knees. Her arms, restrained behind her back, were tethered to the interior of the cage. Her blonde hair was smeared with streaks of dried blood.

Joe jabbed her with the wooden rod again. "Don't you dare pass out on me!"

The basement had only slightly more head clearance than a crawl space, forcing Babu to crawl into the room. "The Boss, she told me to bring a rabbit for dinner."

"Well, we better get you cleaned up, then." Joe reached for the pull-cord of the pressure washer.

Babu grimaced as Rhian's cries of torment filled his head. He moved into the space between Joe and his victim. The jet stream tore the back of his shirt.

"Get out of the way, dummy!"

Babu unlatched the door of the cage. "Sorry lade-la-little rabbit."

He yanked the rope free from the anchor point and carefully unwrapped her raw wrists. Babu knelt and scooped her up to carry her.

Rhian peered at him through swollen eyes. "Thank you."

As The Boss looked in the mirror of her vanity, she saw Joe enter her room. She continued to run the brush through her thick, black hair. "Hey, Joe, what do you know?"

"Your *Dragon* and *Viper* have arrived. They're downstairs in your office."

She gave her reflection a slight smile, then parted her lips as she smeared them with lipstick. "I want you to wear that suit I had tailored for you tonight. We need to look our best."

The Boss stood from the cushioned stool at the vanity. She began to untie her lace robe as she sauntered across the room. She took cover behind the dressing room screen and dropped her robe to the floor. Her silhouette revealed her motions as she unrolled her stockings to her thigh and clipped them to the garter.

The Boss stepped out from behind the privacy of the screen. She wore a long, form-fitting white dress with a slit up one side that revealed her black stockings.

"Would you mind?" She turned her bare back to Joe. He approached and gently raised the long zipper to secure the dress.

"I want to keep her," he said.

"You just *had* to remind me of your obsession with her. Your pernicious habit of lusting over young women ends now. You men are all the same. Why, your very lives have been spared at their cost, and yet you still think they owe you something. You will leave *my* Rabbit alone, Joe. I mean it."

"She would have loved me. I was just getting through to her when Babu took her from me!"

"You were *getting through to her?*"

"Yeah, Boss, you know, I was trying to—"

"Bring her to me."

"But, Boss—"

"Now, Joe!"

The moonlight painted the warehouse in a shade of blue that only midnight could offer. Skewed checkerboard designs were cast across the floor by the grids of the transom windows.

Babu led Drake and Veronica to the large dining table centralized on the warehouse floor. The formal setting was dressed with elegance. The rose-gold flatware and crystal glasses sparkled in the candlelight.

"Have a sit."

Drake and Veronica took the seats assigned by Babu. Drake waited until he had left them, and then he leaned toward Veronica.

"Just stick to the plan."

"I don't know about this, Drake. How do you know she will kill him?"

"You weren't there. She said it herself that they had *unfinished business.*"

"You're sure she'll make a deal with us to get Kranes back?"

"She won't have a choice; he's the only surgeon left."

Veronica scanned the table. "This better not be just for show. I'm starving."

"Excuse me, Waiter." Drake raised his hand. "Can we get a basket of rolls to start?"

Veronica laughed. "If only it were that easy."

"With Miles out of the way, no one at The Red Tent will go hungry again."

Veronica smiled. "I love you."

"I love you too."

The Boss was arranging an assortment of daisies in a vase. She removed one from the bunch and slid it behind her ear. *Perfect.*

"Here she is." Joe released his hold of Rhian's arm.

The Boss turned, taking in the sight of Rhian's ravaged body. "What have you done?"

"He painted my roses red." Rhian moaned.

The Boss glared at Joe. "Go make sure the men are ready to receive our guest of honor."

"Off with their heads," Rhian added in a shaken voice.

"Come on, dear. I may have a dress that will fit you." The Boss took Rhian's hands, pulled her into an embrace, and placed a delicate kiss on top of her head.

Backing away, The Boss looked at Rhian's bruised face. "What do you think about making this party a masquerade?"

"Will there be tea?"

———————————————————————

"Do you remember when I fell behind in school?" Lawrence turned back to face Becker.

He was several paces behind. "This is nothing like med school."

"You're slow, that's all I'm saying." Lawrence laughed. "Does Jane even know you're on this little field trip?"

"I appreciate you coming, Lawrence. Just do me a favor and stop talking." Becker pressed the release lever and bolted forward to catch up.

The warehouse shared the same characteristics as the men guarding it. Both had thrived in past years, forgotten—both had refused to die. They didn't die, and yet, what The Boss had done to them left them more undead than alive. Now they only knew servitude.

Lawrence motioned that they should take cover. "We need to wait for backup, Matt."

"How do you know that Marshall followed through with The Guardian order?"

"Do you think he'd miss out on the opportunity to take down Angeline? An eye for an eye, as they say."

"Then we need to get in there before Marshall does. He'll kill everyone to get to her."

"See those rifles they're holding? They fire forty-five rounds per minute. I'd be more worried about *them* killing *us* if I were you."

"We walked all this way for the wheel to charge. It will only lose power the longer we wait. It's time I find out if I'm faster than a speeding bullet."

Lawrence pulled his gun from its holster. "I've got fifteen rounds to help you live out this fantasy, Becker. Then you're on your own."

Becker plotted his course. He had no idea how to turn at full speed; he imagined he would have to stop and reset. Two guards at the entrance. Four along the street. One at the open roll-up door around the back. Becker went over it again. *Four on the street is a straight shot. I could take out the one at the rear after. That still leaves the two up front.*

"Just make sure the two at the entrance don't retreat inside."

"What's the plan?" Lawrence felt a breeze as Becker passed by. *Okay, good talk.*

One. Becker reached down as he approached the first guard. He took hold of the rifle; the strap tugged at the man's shoulder, causing him to twist. The pivoting motion of the action demanded too much from the guard's knee. *Torn anterior cruciate ligament.* Becker continued on.

Two. The second guard hadn't yet noticed him. Again, Becker reached for the gun. No strap. He felt the guard's firm grip on the weapon. Becker twisted the weapon in his hand. *Volar plate avulsion fracture. Hopefully, he's not ambidextrous.*

Three. The guard turned at the oncoming commotion. He lowered his weapon and held out his hand to brace against the hit. Becker took hold of his left arm. *Open compound fracture.* The blood splatter missed Becker as he rushed past.

Four. The final guard on the street, then he'd need to stop and reset. His gun was pointed, but Becker's adrenaline had already alerted him to this. He threw the lever back to neutral with a quick motion of his thumb. The sudden loss of power in his legs caused him to stumble and fall forward. The rifle was pointed too high as Becker struck the guard in his midsection. The guard's feet came out from under him, and he fell, the back of his head striking the ground. *Cervical vertebrae break.* Becker felt for a pulse. *Thank God.*

The rear guard rounded the corner of the building. "Hands up!"

Becker strained to stand and face him; he did as he was told. *I must get closer.* He stepped toward the man, whose weapon was unwavering.

"It's nothing personal, Doc, but I gotta bring you to her." The guard motioned to Becker to turn around.

"What does she have on you?" Becker kept closing the distance.

The guard looked at his crippled comrades, each with his own distinctive cry of anguish.

He lowered his rifle. "She saved our lives."

"You don't believe that?" Becker reached for the gun.

"She'll kill me."

"Then go, just leave. Get out of here!"

The guard jerked away and readied his weapon.

Becker was prepared. *Five.* He pushed the second lever forward, transferring the last of the stored energy to his arms. Each punch found the guard's face with devastating accuracy. *Mandibular fracture. Nasal fracture.*

The flywheel slowed to a stop; Becker collapsed to the ground. The guard joined him, falling just beside him. Becker looked at the young man's hammered face. *The floor of the eye socket is so thin in many places. I've broken it.* He looked away from the bulging, bloody eye.

Six. Seven. Becker heard what must have been two shots from Lawrence's pistol. *Not what I had in mind.* He slid across the sidewalk to turn back and see if his assumption was right. At the other end of the building, Lawrence held his hands out to the side and shrugged at Becker.

"A little help here?" Becker called.

The gunshots had captured her attention. The Boss held the wineglass to her lips, frozen as she listened. "He's here."

Babu stabbed his fork into his steak and brought it to his mouth as if it were a drumstick. The rest of the dinner party had paused at The Boss's words.

"Babu, when you're not too busy, bring me the doctor." Babu took another bite. "I meant now. Dr. Becker. Remember?"

The Boss raised an eyebrow. Babu lifted the tablecloth to wipe his face. The guests grabbed at the candles to steady them from the motion.

Lawrence nearly dropped Becker as he loosened his hold to open the door. "Worst plan ever."

Babu saw the men in the moonlit doorway and quickened his pace. Lawrence lowered Becker to the floor inside. He shut his eyes as Babu reached them. *Worst plan ever.* Babu took a hold of his face, squeezing his temples between his thumb and pinky finger. *Worst plan ever!* Babu released Lawrence as he passed out.

The Boss held an unlit cigarette with idle fingers and smiled as Babu returned with Becker over his shoulder. "Seat him there, at the end of the table." She gestured with her smoke.

Becker fell limply onto the chair. "The irony isn't lost on me, Samantha."

"Excuse me?"

"Your sister died because her lungs were infected, and you have chosen to smoke. Cigarettes kill more than four hundred eighty thousand people a year."

Drake erupted in laughter. "You need to get updated statistics, Doctor. There aren't even that many people left alive!"

"And yet, you all have survived," Becker said.

Rhian looked at The Boss and back at Becker. "Curiouser and curiouser."

"Oh, how rude of me." The Boss stood from the table. "Let's see, to your left, we have Dragon, Viper, and Joe."

Becker followed the introductions with his eyes.

"My name is Samantha, but everyone knows to call me The Boss." She stood opposite Becker and tipped her large-brimmed hat.

"Then we have Babu and Rabbit, and the empty seat there is for Dr. Kranes. He couldn't make it this evening."

Becker sat up in his seat. "I've had enough of this masquerade."

"You heard the good doctor. Masks off, then." The Boss looked at the guests.

Drake and Veronica did as they were told. Rhian bowed her head. "I was told there would be tea," she whined, and then followed suit.

Drake leaned in to Becker. "Something wrong with your hearing?"

"Please." Becker looked past Drake to Veronica and back. "I may be able to help you, you and your baby."

"She said masks off!" Drake lunged forward and pulled off Becker's mask.

Becker felt his lungs draw in the unfiltered air. *You were right, Lawrence. Worst plan ever.* "Who will perform your surgeries if I become infected, Samantha?"

The Boss was paralyzed with rage. Joe stood, knocking his chair back from the table. He revealed his revolver and aimed it at Drake, ready for the order.

"Dr. Kranes will continue his work." Drake blew off the mounting attack and reclaimed his seat.

The Boss circled the table and stood behind Drake. She placed her hand on his shoulder. "Do you know where Dr. Kranes is?"

Drake grinned. "Why, yes, Samantha, I do."

Veronica glanced up at The Boss. "You can't save Becker without him, and we won't give him to you unless he dies."

Drake glared. "You'll die either way, Dr. Becker!"

Becker placed his hands on the table and pushed himself up to stand. "I will die knowing you all had a second chance to be—"

The generator started, and the overhead lights flickered on.

Joe turned his gun on Becker. "It's a setup!" He pulled the trigger. The bullet struck his chest, sending Becker back onto his chair. He gasped for air, clutching at his chest. Then he fell face-first to the floor and lay there unconscious, with blood dripping from his wound.

Marshall noted the sudden illumination from within the building. "That's our signal. I want groups of three around each side. Sanchez, Jackson, you're with me at the rear. You're brave men and women for being here. 'And do not fear those who kill the body but cannot kill the soul. Rather, fear him who can destroy both soul and body in hell.'"

The large Guardian force did a final check of their weapons and set off toward the building.

Lawrence regained his footing. Starting up the generator had been an exhausting effort. He brought his hands up to cup either side of his throbbing head. He squinted in pain. *What a headache.* He doubled back toward the main room and quickly took cover behind the printing press.

"Now, now, boys, let's be fair." The Boss pulled the daisy out from behind her ear. She removed one petal at a time. "We kill him, we kill him not . . . "

Lawrence hit the power switch on the idle printing press. It spat out fliers: ORGAN TRANSPLANTS. ORGAN TRANSPLANTS. ORGAN TRANSPLANTS.

The distraction allowed Lawrence to lay hold of Rhian and flee the warehouse.

The Boss stopped reciting and listened to the press. *Organ transplants.* She had to choose who lived and who died. But some hadn't had that choice. She thought of her sister. *It wasn't your fault, Jess. You didn't kill our mother. It should have been you; you should have survived. I'm sorry.*

Drake snatched the flower from her hand. "Just kill him!"

The action broke her from her daze. "Oh, Dragon, you shouldn't have done that."

"Forget the flower. We came here to do one thing, and—" Joe cut Drake's words short as he struck him with the butt of his pistol.

Veronica pushed past Joe. "No!"

Babu grabbed Veronica by the arm, stopping her from reaching Drake. He turned her around and closed his arms around her chest. The Boss nodded toward the exit.

Babu entered the rear loading area of the warehouse, where the car was waiting. He saw a man offering his jacket to Rhian as they stepped outside. Babu nodded to Lawrence. "Take the girl and run."

Lawrence saw the large man struggling to keep hold of Veronica. He carefully pushed her into the back of the car. Lowering himself to sit next to her, Babu rested his arm on her shoulders. He pulled Veronica from the window into his chest as she sobbed.

Joe took the driver's seat. "What's going on, Boss?"

"Just drive, Joe."

The car sputtered to a start. Joe flipped on the headlights and let the car roll into the alleyway.

Indeed, under the law, almost everything is purified with blood, and without the shedding of blood there is no forgiveness of sins. Marshall signaled to open fire.

Shots came with relentless fury, pelting the car. The driver's-side panels were shredded with holes, the tires flat. Windows were blown out. Joe sustained several shots to the chest and head, and his mutilated body fell forward onto the steering wheel, pressing the horn.

The sound jolted The Boss. She held her left shoulder, where she'd been hit. The attackers were closing in. She reached for Joe's gun. Flipped open the cylinder. *One shot left.*

"You see, Samantha." Sam picked a second flower and held it out to her. "This flower is no less perfect than the one you hold. They're identical in appearance, like you and your sister." Sam plucked a petal from his flower. "But now, this one is different. Flawed. It's not the same as your flower. Do you understand?" Sam took hold of young Samantha's hands, gripping her flower. "You're the only thing that matters to me."

The Boss held the gun to her head. *He loved me.* She pulled the trigger. *He loved me not.* Again. *He loved me.*

The gun flash filled the car.

Babu's bullet-riddled body was heavy on Veronica. She reached for the handle of the door and slid out from under him.

Rhian screamed out at the sight of Veronica crawling from the car: "Don't shoot her!"

That's a good rabbit. Veronica fell to the alley ground.

Lawrence reentered the warehouse. As he swung open the door, Becker fell onto his back from his leaning position.

"Hold on, buddy. I got you."

Lawrence dropped to his knees and pressed his hands over Becker's chest wound. *Tension pneumothorax. A collapsed lung.* Lawrence desperately tried to remember how to treat the injury. "I need a needle!"

After a night on the streets of *Franklin City*, you either woke up to the lights of the hospital, or you were left in the darkness of the morgue.

FREAKLAND CITY